KNIGHTS ACADEMY

THE FORBIDDEN POWER

BY MAX BRALLIER

ILLUSTRATED BY ALESSANDRO VALDRIGHI
AND PAUL LEE

D0181607

SCHOLASTIC INC.

For my parents. You built me a very radical, very unclean LEGO creation room in our damp basement when I was seven years old—and I played for hours upon hours. Thanks for encouraging creativity and valuing play.

Thank you to everyone at the LEGO Group, specifically Paul Hansford, Mikkel Lee, Helle Reimers Holm-Jørgensen, and Peter Moorby; thanks for allowing me to play and create in such a wonderful world. This is a childhood dream come true. Thanks to Debra Dorfman, Samantha Schutz, Michael Petranek, Rick DeMonico, Elizabeth Schaefer, and everyone at Scholastic—thank you for inviting me in and welcoming me and being a delight to work with. As always, Dan Lazar for putting this together and Torie Doherty-Munro for being generally awesome. Above all, thank you to my wife, Alyse, for being the best, always.
—Max Brallier

ISBN 978-1-338-04183-5 (TRADE)   ISBN 978-1-338-16385-8 (SSE)

10 9 8 7 6 5 4 3 2 1   17 18 19 20 21

Printed in the U.S.A.   23

First printing 2017

Book design by Rick DeMonico

CHAPTER ONE

Fletcher Bowman was nervous.

No, not just nervous. Poison ivy made Fletcher nervous. The dentist made Fletcher nervous.

Right now, Fletcher was more than nervous. Fletcher was anxious, agitated, apprehensive, and straight-up *scared*.

He was sitting on a cold, cracked seat on the holorail. The blue-and-gold train car was zipping toward the great city of Knightonia, speeding down the shimmering blue ribbon-rails. Fletcher had been riding the train for three straight days: His bottom was sore, and his neck was stiff. He didn't have the money for one of the train's fancy sleeping cars, so he'd been in the same not-so-comfy seat for seventy-two straight hours.

He was finally nearing his destination, though that wasn't bringing him much relief . . .

There was a crackling sound. Then a voice came over the speaker: *"Next stop: Knights' Academy."*

Fletcher pressed his face to the window. Nearly everything was a blur as the train sped into Knightonia, whirring past glowing beam bridges and the state-of-the-art Joustdome. Huge, high-tech brick buildings dotted the horizon. The city seemed endlessly huge.

Fletcher clutched his traveling bag as the holo-rail shuddered, hissed, and slowed. The conductor marched down the aisle. "Knights' Academy! Now arriving!"

Fletcher stood up. Brushing his shaggy brown hair out from over his eyes, he noticed that he was the *only* person to stand up. Apparently, very few students took public transportation to the academy.

The train came to a smooth stop, and the doors slid open. As Fletcher approached the exit, a voice barked, "Hey! Kid!"

Fletcher turned to see the conductor holding his travel bag. "This yours?"

Fletcher was so anxious, agitated, apprehensive, and

straight-up *scared* that he had nearly left his bag—*every last thing he possessed*—on the holo-rail.

"Oh yes! Thank you!" Fletcher said. "I'm sorry, it's my first time in the city, and I'm just a little—"

Fletcher was interrupted by the conductor heaving the heavy traveling bag. Fletcher's eyes burst wide open, and—

OOF!

The bag punched Fletcher in the chest. He managed to catch it—*sort of.* Imagine trying to snag a hefty grunting hog, midflight. That's how Fletcher caught his bag. It *plowed* into him, and it knocked him right off the train car. He hit the ground, tumbled over backward twice, and finally came to a stop, one leg in the air, sprawled out, on the grass.

Fletcher managed to squeak out a pained "Thanks . . ."

The holo-rail squealed and glided on down the tracks. Watching it go, Fletcher's stomach felt hollow—like it had been way too long since he'd eaten. It was his nerves. He wanted to jump back on the train. He wanted to slide into his seat, lower his head, and ride the train all the way home.

He was homesick, and he'd only been in Knightonia for, like, 3.8 seconds.

He was homesick—and he didn't even particularly *like* home!

"Off to a great start . . ." Fletcher mumbled as he picked up his bag and got to his feet.

The first thing Fletcher *really* noticed was this: The city stunk. He didn't mean it figuratively, like "Oh, Knightonia is the *worst*."

No. It literally stinks, Fletcher thought. *Like, it smells. It smells like swarms of people and jam-packed streets and grease and crowded malls and hustle and bustle.*

Fletcher had never traveled more than a few miles from his home, the orphanage outside the fishing village of Salty Town. Now he was *thousands* of miles from home, in the biggest city in the realm.

A rising tide of chatter and conversation caused Fletcher to turn. He saw it for the first time: the Knights' Academy.

The Knights' Academy.

It was huge and towering. A brick pathway led to a large gate, with a glowing blue shield in the center. Light from massive pixel torches sparkled and danced.

Fletcher couldn't believe how many students there were: hundreds scattered across the bright green lawn that surrounded the academy walls. Some got hugs and kisses from parents. Others greeted friends.

But not Fletcher Bowman.

Fletcher was alone, on the outside, watching. There was no one to hug him good-bye or give him a pat on the back and say, "Good luck."

Fletcher had lived at the orphanage since he was a baby. It was the only life he knew. The orphanage was on the seaside in the Rocklands, where the land was dry but the smell of the sea hung in the air, always. He was one of twenty-seven orphans there, and he worked at the orphanage every day. Every weekend, he made the forty-five-minute trek into Salty Town and did *more* work, helping out at the salt farmers' market. The town was nothing special, but Fletcher liked it. It was busy— at least, Fletcher had *thought* it was busy. It was nothing like this . . .

There was one old Holovision screen at the orphanage, so Fletcher had learned a little bit about the NEXO KNIGHTS heroes, and he of course knew about Knightonia. But the big city had always felt so far away. Now it was right here, in front of him . . .

He sighed. "Here goes nothing."

But as Fletcher took his first step toward the academy, there was a sudden—

BURRUP-BURRUP-BRA-BROOOOOO!

It was the single loudest sound Fletcher had ever heard. So loud, in fact, it startled him.

Startled would be a nice way to put it. In fact, Fletcher was so scared he dropped his bag, jumped, did a goofy half turn, and sort of kicked out his leg.

A few nearby students saw and laughed. Fletcher felt his face turning pink. One boy, with a bronzed face and slick black hair, laughed loudest.

"Never heard a carriage horn before?" the boy called.

Fletcher had promised himself he'd do his best not to be shy or intimidated, so he reluctantly dragged his bag over to the students. There were two boys, both of them in crisp clothes. Fletcher suddenly felt self-conscious. His pants were ripped, and his coat was stained. He had tried to clean his shirt before he left the orphanage—he had spent two days scrubbing—but now it just looked overscrubbed and worn.

"Sure, I've heard a carriage horn," Fletcher said, doing his best to sound cheerful. "But that sounded like a monster-sized trumpet or something."

The boys snickered. "That's 'cause that's the Richmond carriage," the boy with slick black hair said. "It's all gold and pulled by hover horses."

Looking down, Fletcher saw both boys had clean, fancy rolling suitcases. Fletcher glanced at his own bag—covered in tape and patches and stray threads. Ignoring that, he quickly stuck out his hand. "My name's Fletcher Bowman."

The slick-haired boy looked at Fletcher's hand with barely-hidden disgust, but after a moment, he shook it. "I'm Ethan Zilgo. And this is Beak," he said, jerking a thumb at the tall, wiry, redheaded boy beside him.

Just then, a chorus of "oohs" and "aahs" spread through the crowd. The carriage door was opening.

"That will be Lance . . ." Beak said.

Fletcher had a habit of blurting things out when he was nervous—and he now blurted, "Who's Lance?"

Zilgo and Beak glared at Fletcher. They were observing him like he was the human embodiment of a skin rash.

"Lance *Richmond*," Zilgo said.

"The most *famous* knight in the land . . ." Beak said.

"From the most famous *family* in the land . . ." Zilgo added.

Fletcher was oblivious—he had *zero* clue who Lance Richmond was. But there was no way he could let on, so he lied . . .

"Oh right! Of course!" Fletcher said quickly. "*Lance* Richmond! I thought you said, um . . ."

The boys continued staring at Fletcher. Fletcher hoped they'd stop looking so he could stop talking, but as long as they kept gawking at him, he kept blabbing. "I thought you said, uh, something else."

"Something else?" Zilgo asked.

Fletcher felt big globs of sweat beginning to drip down his forehead. "Yeah. Um. Pants. *Pants* Richmond."

"Pants Richmond?" Beak asked.

Fletcher knew this was not the most perfect lie he had ever told.

Zilgo and Beak gawked at Fletcher like his brain was possibly broken. And the longer they stared at him, the worse Fletcher felt. Fletcher had shown up anxious, agitated, apprehensive, and straight-up *scared*. And everything he was afraid of going wrong had gone wrong in, like, seven seconds. Fletcher felt his face turning bright red. He tried to tell his face to *stop* turning red, but that just made it worse.

And before he knew what was happening, Fletcher was running away. Really. Just flat-out *sprinting*.

"Where are you hurrying off to?" Zilgo hollered.

On the *inside*, Fletcher was screaming at himself. *Why are you running? Where are you going?*

Fletcher had done one silly thing—and he was already running for cover! Like, literally *running* for *cover*.

Fletcher slipped behind a wide oak tree.

"That weird commoner kid just hid behind a tree!" he heard Beak cry out. "Guess you scared him, Zilgo!"

Great start, Fletcher thought as he caught his breath. He knocked his head against the tree. "Stupid, stupid, stupid!" he told himself.

He was here to become a knight—a knight! And he was already so embarrassed that he had to cower behind a tree? Not very knightly!

The truth was, Fletcher wasn't sure he *wanted* to be a knight. One week earlier, the orphanage headmaster had simply said, "Fletcher. You're now old enough to attend Knights' Academy. So now you *will* attend Knights' Academy." And that was that. It came out of nowhere! Fletcher had never heard of the *other* orphans being sent to Knights' Academy. But Fletcher had no say in the matter—they just sent him on his not-so-merry way . . .

From where he stood now, Fletcher could see the holo-rail track. All he had to do was march over there, get on the holo-rail, and it would take him back to the orphanage. It would whisk him away from this embarrassment and all this overwhelming *newness*. He could tell the headmaster that—hmm—they already had too many knights or something. They ran out of swords! Or they were all booked up—no more rooms at the academy!

A voice boomed, interrupting Fletcher's planning. "Fans! My public! It is *so* wonderful to see you all!"

Fletcher peeked around the tree. Fletcher now recognized the knight that now stood in front of the carriage. Fletcher had seen him on Holovision. He was Lance

Richmond. The knight's voice thundered like an actor's onstage.

The well-groomed, blond-haired Lance Richmond was soaking up the attention of the adoring crowd: smiling, flashing big pearly whites, and handing out autographed photos of himself. "It is *lovely* to see you. I wish I could spend *hours* gracing you with my presence. But today I'm only here to drop off Isabella. But please, have a photo—they're signed!"

Who's Isabella? Fletcher wondered.

Students and parents were pushing and shoving to get a glimpse.

"Where's your sister?" one student shouted.

"Probably waiting for the Squireazzi to show up and snap some pics!" a parent responded.

But it was Fletcher who was the first to spot Isabella Richmond. He saw a flash of silver-blond hair, and the girl's resemblance to Lance was instantly apparent. It was Isabella, but she was most definitely *not* waiting for the Squireazzi.

She was on her hands and knees, wriggling through the crowd. When she stood, muck dripped from her hands. She looked at her palms, shrugged, and wiped them on her once-white pants.

Fletcher grinned. She might have arrived in a golden carriage, but this Isabella didn't seem so fancy.

Suddenly, a group of robots spotted her sneaking away.

"Oh boy, the Squireazzi are on her!" someone shouted.

Fletcher saw the blond girl groan and kick her feet. She dragged a large, fancy luggage case behind her as she dashed across the grass. And—*oh man*—she was running toward the tree! Toward his hiding place!

Fletcher whipped his head back around the tree. *Don't come back here, don't come back here, don't come back here, don't come back here.*

She came back there . . .

Isabella burst around the side of the tree, tried to stop, skidded, and splatted on the ground. Fletcher, without even knowing what he was doing, stuck out his hand and helped her to her feet.

"Thanks, kid," Isabella said, smiling warmly. She wore red beam glasses and the high-tech frames were dotted with bits of mud. "So whatcha doing back here? Just hiding behind a tree? That's normal."

"Um . . ." Fletcher started.

"You mind if I hide, too?" Isabella interrupted.

"Um . . ."

"Fantastic, thanks. The Squireazzi are the *worst*."

Fletcher was about to ask what Squireazzi were, when Zilgo and Beak appeared. Their eyes were wide,

and their mouths hung open. They stared at Isabella—both dumbstruck *and* starstruck.

Fletcher hated awkward silence, so he said, "I'm Fletcher. Fletcher Bowman. So, Isabella, you're, like, ah, *famous* or something?"

Zilgo then roared, "Of *course* she's famous! She's a *Richmond*! What did you come to Knights' Academy for if you don't know anything about knights!?"

Fletcher shrugged. "Well, I didn't really have a choice . . . I'm an orphan. They just sent me on my way."

Isabella eyeballed Zilgo for a moment, then said, "Slick hair. Beach tan. You must be a Zilgo."

The boy stuck out his chin, puffed out his chest, and nodded proudly. "That's right. Ethan Zilgo."

Isabella stared at Ethan Zilgo a moment longer, then turned to Fletcher. "An orphan, huh? Buddy, sometimes I *wish* I was an orphan. This Richmond last name stiiiinks. My brother just *had* to drop me off for the first day of school. It's the *worst*."

Zilgo and Beak now stared, still dumbfounded, at both Isabella *and* Fletcher. They had confused looks all over their faces. Why was *she* chatting with *him*?

KA-KLANG!

The large front gates were opening—and just in time. A squad of Squireazzi was hurrying toward them, waving cameras and microphones. Isabella tugged on Fletcher's sleeve. "Come on!" she said, sprinting ahead.

Fletcher grabbed his bag and did his best to carry it with one hand. He didn't want to look weak. Knights weren't exactly known for lacking strength.

"Isabella, wait up!" Fletcher called.

She suddenly stopped and spun, her blue eyes *boring* into Fletcher's. "One thing," she said. "Do *not* call me Isabella, 'kay? I *hate* that name. It's too fancy and formal. And now that I'm at school, away from my parents, I can *finally* ditch it. I go by Izzy. Got it?"

"Izzy," Fletcher said, nodding. "Got it."

Izzy grinned. "Goodie. And—hmmm—*Fletcher*. That's your name, huh?"

Fletcher nodded again. He realized Izzy talked in a way that left him doing a lot of nodding.

"You like that name?" she asked.

"Well, I never really thought about it. It's just a name."

"A name's a big thing," said Izzy. "And here's the *great* thing about Knights' Academy. It's a new beginning! Now's the time for you to make your future and be who you want to be."

Fletcher had never thought about it like that.

"Really, I just think that name is too long," Izzy said, interrupting his holo-train of thought. *"Fletcher. Fletcherrrrr.* What if we get into a battle with a bunch of Monstrox's minions and I need to call on you for backup? I'll waste, like, precious seconds yelling *'Fletcherrrrr.'* How about just . . . Fletch?"

"Fletch?" he asked.

Izzy nodded. "I think you're a Fletch. You want to be a Fletch?"

Fletcher's mind raced. A nickname? No one had ever given him a nickname.

"Yes," he said finally. "I am *Fletch.*"

With that, they made their way through the gates, into the green-grassed courtyard. Fletch saw the academy's large stone doors opening. For the moment, Fletch's generally anxious, agitated, apprehensive, and straight-up *scared* feelings were replaced with excitement.

CHAPTER TWO

A small gray robot held open the large doors. In a mechanical voice, the robot said, "This way, students. Quickly. No delay."

Fletch gawked at the short silver-and-gray robot. There were almost no robots in Salty Town. "What is that thing?" Fletch whispered, hurrying to catch up. "Is that like those little dudes that were chasing you?"

"Yep. A Squirebot," Izzy said. "They're all over the academy. Can't do a backflip without landing on one. They do just about every job: soldiers, reporters, trumpeters, mechanics, you name it."

The students followed the Squirebot's instructions, stepping up the stone steps. Fletch's heart raced as he shuffled inside, sticking close to Izzy.

Fletch sucked in a small gasp of air as he craned his neck to take in the enormous Entrance Hall.

It was just the entryway, but Fletch was already awestruck.

Two massive winding staircases snaked down from the second floor. Glowing blue shields adorned the walls. Lavish chandeliers, along with holo-banners, high-tech view screens, and buzzing lanterns, all caused the hall to glow with warm blue light. The walls were sparkling white stone, and every inch of the hall was impeccably clean. Fletch thought it looked like, funny enough, the whole hall had just brushed its teeth and showered to prepare for their arrival.

Thinking back to the small, lantern-lit orphanage that he had called home for his entire life, Fletch was breathless. Things had changed . . .

In the center of the hall, overlooking everything, was an immense statue of an armored knight. Fletch shut his eyes, waited a moment, then reopened them—just to make sure it was real.

It was most certainly was. A plaque identified the subject of the statue as Ned Knightley.

"Welcome, first-year students!" a voice boomed.

Fletch gasped. Even *he* recognized the man coming down the staircase. It was King Halbert, ruler of Knighton. He wore a huge smile on his face, only partly hidden beneath his bushy brown beard.

"Holy cow," Fletch said. "That's the king! King Halbert!"

"Sure," Izzy said. "You've never met him?"

"Um. *No.* He's the king."

"Oh. Nice guy. He came to my eighth birthday party."

"This year's class is our biggest in many, many years," King Halbert said. "As you know, the threat of monsters means our once-peaceful kingdom is now very much in need of knights. That is why I, your king, have come to greet you. Also, because I love greetings!"

A few students chuckled.

"Someday, I hope to meet each and every one of you," King Halbert continued, "but for now, I will hand the proceedings to Principal Brickland."

There was a hiss as a door opened, and a gruff-looking man came whooshing in. He sucked all the warm, welcoming air out of the room. His battle boots thudded against the tiled floor as he marched toward the students. Fletch saw scars on his face. He had a thick gray-and-white beard—and Fletch guessed even more scars hid beneath it. *I bet this guy has seen some serious stuff,* Fletch thought.

"Students, leave your bags right where they are," Principal Brickland barked, getting right down to business. "Squirebots will bring them to your dormitory rooms. But don't get used to that sort of treatment."

A thud echoed through the hall as a hundred bags were simultaneously dropped.

"I'm sure you're all quite excited for the big welcome banquet, yes?" Brickland said with a surprising smile.

Just as they began to reply, Brickland's smile vanished, and he roared, "Well, *THERE IS NO WELCOME BANQUET*! You are knights-in-training! You eat when there is *time* to eat. From here on out, your lives will be dedicated to studying, battling, and studying how to battle. You will train *hard*. You will learn *fast*."

"Ooh, fun!" Izzy whispered happily. Fletch, on the other hand, was disappointed that the whole banquet thing wasn't happening. Total fake-out.

"Your first day at Knights' Academy begins with a field-*quest*," Brickland continued as he tapped a large holo-monitor behind him. It blinked to life, and an instant later, a 3-D rendering of a long silver sword appeared.

"This is Ned Knightley's Silver Sword of Silverness. Your quest: *Find it!* It is somewhere on the academy grounds. But is it inside the school? Outside the school? On top of the school? That is for *you* to find out!"

Fletch heard sarcastic grumbling. He turned to see Ethan Zilgo murmur, "Oh, a scavenger hunt? How wonderfully heroic . . ."

Brickland's eyes shot over to Zilgo. He watched him for a moment, then continued. "But I warn you, do *not* leave the academy grounds. The world outside these walls has never been more dangerous. Monstrox and his dark magic roam the land. As knights-in-training, you are *all* my responsibility. Leaving academy grounds will result in quick, no-questions-asked *expulsion*."

Not much earlier, when he was trembling behind the tree, there was a part of Fletch that would have been okay with expulsion. It would have sent him home to his familiar-but-not-fun life at the orphanage. Sure, life at the orphanage was about as exciting as watching armor rust—but at least it was safe! At least it didn't leave him shaking with anxiety!

But now? Now the idea of expulsion was horrifying. Fletch was excited. Nervous, sure, but excited—his entire body tingled with anticipation.

Brickland walked down the line, eyeing the students. "And this is *not* a 'scavenger hunt.'"

Zilgo gulped. Clearly, Principal Brickland didn't miss much.

Brickland continued. "Squirebots and professors hold clues and hints to the whereabouts of Ned Knightley's Silver Sword of Silverness. They will help you . . . *if* they're in the mood. Now partner up. Groups of two—no more, no less. A knight must always be able to rely on the support of his or her fellow knights."

Instantly, Fletch was filled with heart-rattling anxiety. Was there *anything* worse than being asked to partner up?

Fletch swallowed softly and turned to Izzy. He gave her a hopeful shrug, letting her know that, maybe, y'know, *no biggie,* but if she wouldn't mind, perchance they could be partners. Just possibly perhaps?

Izzy glanced at Fletcher, caught his eye, frowned, and then quickly looked off to the crowd of students. Under her breath, she said, "Who should I partner with? Someone smart, someone clever, someone who's had a haircut in the past nine years . . ."

Fletch swallowed hard, and he felt his chin begin to tremble. He had hoped Izzy might be a friend—but he had been wrong. All around him, he heard other students finding partners, laughing, and making new friends. Probably new lifelong companions—bosom buddies, BFFs, soul mates, junk like that.

Fletch stared down at his feet—he half hoped they might just start walking and carry him away from the awful awkwardness that was "partner up."

Partner up. PARTNER UP? Why would anyone ever ask anyone to partner up? It was torture! It was designed to inflict pain upon the weak—that's what it was. Fletch guessed Principal Brickland was culling the herd. Any moment, Brickland would notice Fletch had no partner; Brickland would then shame him in front of everyone and announce that partnering up was an important knight skill or some crud. Fletch would be on the train back to the orphanage in approximately six minutes— he *knew* it.

But when he looked up, Izzy was staring straight at him, a mammoth grin on her face. "Fletch, dude, *really*?" she said. "I'm just jerking your chain mail! Kiddo, you are *way too easy* to mess with."

Fletch raised his eyebrows. "You mean . . . ?"

"Yeah, duh, *of course partners*. Now come on, we've got a sword to find and a field-quest to complete! I *don't* plan on losing—especially not to Zilgo . . ."

Fletch did his best to conceal his giddiness. A moment later, he and Izzy were racing down the warm, bright halls of the Knights' Academy. The windows hummed with blue energy, and a long red carpet reminded Fletch of how *royal* the whole thing felt.

But there was no time for Fletch to soak in the splendid scenery—they were hunting for their first clue . . .

"How do we even know where to begin?" Fletch wondered aloud. "The academy is *huge*."

"We've got an advantage," Izzy said as she flashed a rascally smile. "I used to visit Lance when he was a student. I bet I've spent more time at this school than any other first-year. I know this place like the back of my hand. And me and the back of my hand are *pretty, pretty tight*."

With that, Izzy ducked down a narrow hall, then dashed up a winding flight of stairs. "Keep up!"

Fletch did his best as Izzy sped along, but he found it

hard to follow, since he was constantly craning his neck to take it all in. He could hardly believe how big and busy the academy was. It was an endless maze of hallways, and every corner seemed to hide some ancient piece of armor, legendary weapon, flashing screen, or at-attention Squirebot. The academy gave the impression of a sort of enormous puzzle box, full of secrets, wonders, and mysteries that a student could spend years exploring.

Despite the strict supervision of Principal Brickland, the academy was neither quiet nor calm—just the opposite. School was already in session for the older students, and from every classroom came the sounds of learning and discussion. Fletch's nervous heart was filled with delight—he had never before felt that the world could offer *so much*. It was abuzz with the promise of possibility.

He saw students of all colors and backgrounds, hailing from every corner of Knighton: from Auremville to the Hill Country. He passed professors with peculiar accents who dressed in fashions he'd never seen. He inhaled the scents of humming energy, greased weaponry, freshly oiled armor, and—

Wait, Fletch thought. *The scent of* jackrabbit stew?

Izzy skated to a sudden, inelegant stop—slipping, tripping, then nearly banging into a locker. They had come to the academy kitchen—and Fletch did indeed smell the rich aroma of jackrabbit stew.

Izzy lifted her hand to her mouth. "Shh. I hear Zilgo."

They carefully peeked around the corner. Fletch saw Zilgo and Beak were speaking with someone— and Zilgo seemed to be cornering the man.

"That's Chef Munch," Izzy whispered, adjusting her glasses. "*Best* mince pie in Knightonia. Also, dope milk shakes."

Brushing his hair from over his ears, Fletch could just barely pick up the conversation.

Beak spoke, "Zilgo, I *told* you. This guy's just a cook! He doesn't know anything. He's not a knight, professor, or even a squire."

Zilgo said to his friend, "These simple working types often know more than you'd expect."

Chef Munch shook his head. His pot of jackrabbit stew—which had Fletch's stomach growling—was about to boil over, and Chef Munch looked eager to get back to it. "I don't know anything about a field-quest," the chef said. "Now beat it, before I tell Principal Brickland what nuisances you first-year students are."

"You would inform Brickland?" Zilgo said, opening his palm, revealing the shimmer of gold and silver. "Even after we offered you *money*?"

"He's bribing him!" Fletch whispered angrily.

"Why, that little . . ." Izzy rolled up her sleeves, balled up her hands, and was about to storm in when Fletch hooked her collar.

"Hold on," Fletch said. "Maybe we'll get a hint!"

Chef Munch hesitantly eyed the money. After a moment, he said, "I saw Brickland on the training grounds, late last night. That's all I know."

Zilgo looked the chef up and down, like he didn't quite believe him. Then he snatched a roll from a pile of bread. "The training grounds, eh?" Zilgo asked, chomping into the bread. "You've been helpful, Chef. But I hoped for more. Here—you get *one* piece of copper."

Fletch whipped his head back around just as Zilgo and Beak made for the door. Hugging the wall, Fletch and Izzy watched Zilgo and Beak burst past them, hurrying down the hall, snickering and proclaiming the usefulness of a little spare change.

Watching Zilgo, Fletch decided he had never come to dislike someone so much in so short an amount of time.

Izzy's arm sprung straight ahead. "Fletch," she said. "To the training grounds! If Zilgo's going to play dirty, we will, too."

"Wait . . . Can we get some bread? It smelled all fresh! And toasty! And doughy!"

Izzy growled. "Training grounds, Fletch, training grounds! I *don't* like to lose . . ."

They were called the training grounds, but they were more like fields: endless lawns, dotted with enormous trees. The grass was so green it practically glowed neon. The clashing sounds of competition filled the air. Students sparred while professors barked out instructions. Swords, axes, maces, lances, and every other imaginable armament hung from weapon racks.

Izzy marched quickly across the neatly trimmed fields, taking sharp turns, in and around the combat. Fletch followed, spinning, turning, trying to take it all in. Pausing to watch two students face off in combat, Fletch saw a student thrust her shield into the air, and suddenly, a golden beam shot upward, pixels appeared, and the beam returned to the shield.

"Whoa!" Fletch exclaimed, hurrying to catch up to Izzy. "Did you see that? That light was just, like, *beamed* down from the sky into that girl's shield. And then her armor and sword started glowing!"

Izzy laughed. "That's a NEXO Power. You know, as in *NEXO KNIGHTS*. A fusion of digital and magic! That's the whole reason we're *here*, Fletch—to learn how to be knights and wield NEXO Powers. NEXO Powers bestow all our cool tech-armor with awesome

monster-fighting capabilities! Powered-up swords, high-tech crossbows—coolness galore!"

"Oh," Fletch said. He felt woefully uninformed about NEXO Powers and the general business of knighting.

"Don't stress it," Izzy said. "You'll catch on! Hopefully . . ."

First-year students scurried about, searching for clues to the whereabouts of Ned Knightley's Silver Sword of Silverness. Some consulted maps. One eyed a glowing tablet. In the distance, a pair examined a possible clue tucked behind a tree.

Fletch spotted Zilgo and Beak attempting to get information from a professor—but the duo didn't appear to be getting far. "I'm in the middle of a lesson on parrying tactics," the professor snapped, "and you dare interrupt me?! *Away!*"

Fletcher and Izzy grinned as Zilgo stomped off, looking embarrassed. "That's Captain Clash, the battle instructor," Izzy said. "Not the friendliest guy. Surprised he didn't fire a dragon arrow at Zilgo."

Fletch wasn't sure what a dragon arrow was—but he was pretty sure Zilgo deserved to have one fired in his general direction.

The sounds of combat faded as Fletch and Izzy approached the far edge of the training grounds. There, a short, round woman stood outside an ivy-covered shed made of crumbling stone and brick. The woman was sharpening an axe blade against a spinning wet stone.

"Izzy Richmond!" the woman called, barely pausing to look their way. "I forgot this was your year!"

"You bet," Izzy said. *"Finally!"*

The woman shut off the spinning stone and examined the axe. It was razor-sharp, and the edge glimmered in the high, afternoon sun. Seemingly satisfied, she set the axe down. "How's your brother?"

"Annoying," Izzy said with a groan.

The woman laughed and then glanced at Fletch, looking him up and down. "Well, you're just all skin and bones, aren't you?" she said. "Don't fret it too much; we feed students well. I'm Brutzle. Kind of a Jack—or rather, Jill—of all trades 'round here."

Before Fletch could stick out his hand, Brutzle snatched it and yanked it up and down. It was the strongest shake Fletch had ever experienced, and his arm felt like rubber when she finally let go. "Very nice to meet you," he squeaked. "I'm Fletch."

Inching close to Brutzle, Izzy said, "We were hoping you might provide us with a clue . . ."

"A clue . . . ?" Brutzle asked, not seeming to understand—and then, just one second later, realizing.

"Right! The first-year's field-quest! Forgot you were on the hunt . . ."

Brutzle dug into her pocket and slipped out a scrap of paper. She cleared her throat, stood up straight, then read in a theatrical voice:

> *A knight that was most legendary, blade held to the sky.*
>
> *Peek closely around the base, a clue there you will spy . . .*

Izzy whistled softly as she pondered the puzzling clue, massaging it, 'round and 'round, and then suddenly exclaiming, "The Hall of Knights! That's it, Brutzle, isn't it?"

"You'll get nothing more from me," the woman replied with a hearty smile. She scooped up a long halberd. "Back to work. Need to keep the swords sharp and the shields shieldy. Especially with Monstrox out there . . ."

Izzy and Fletch thanked Brutzle, and then they were speeding back toward the academy. Ascending a long stone staircase, Fletch had the sudden feeling they were being followed. Glancing behind him, he spotted Zilgo and Beak trying—and failing—to remain inconspicuous. Before Fletch could tell Izzy, she said, "I know. Zilgo's following us. Thinks he's going to ride our coattails to victory."

When they came to a wide hall full of fourth-year classrooms, Izzy said, "What time is it?"

Fletch glanced at a digital clock on the wall. "Two oh five."

Izzy said, "Perfecto," and at that very instant, a trumpet blared. It was the end of the period, Fletch realized, and a dozen doors opened on each side of the hall. In an instant, hundreds of students were pouring from the classrooms.

Izzy sped up, ducking beneath bobbing backpacks and darting past professors. Fletch did his best to follow: right, left, left, right, down a flight of stairs, up a flight of stairs, stepping quickly outside to cross a sun-splashed terrace, and then back inside.

Zilgo and Beak were far, far behind by the time Fletch and Izzy arrived at the Hall of Knights . . .

CHAPTER THREE

"Wow," Fletch said quietly.

Izzy grinned. "I know. Impressive, right?"

They were inside a long gallery, full of large bronze sculptures of legendary knights. Some were posted atop horses. Others stood heroically, with sword and shield. Fletch held his breath as they walked the polished brick floor. The hall reminded him of museums he had read about in books. It seemed endless—with hundreds of sculptures, each huge.

"These are knights from the golden age," Izzy said. "Before digital magic. Before the NEXO Powers. Before Merlok 2.0."

"Merlok 2.0?" Fletch asked.

"Sure—the digital version of Merlok. You *do* know who Merlok is, right?"

"Ahh, sure I do," Fletch said unconvincingly. "But why don't you pretend I *don't* and tell me all about it. Just for kicks . . ."

"Fletch, buddy, you're a terrible liar," Izzy said, laughing. "Merlok 2.0 is the wizard of the OS! Merlok was the last magician in the land. But he sacrificed himself to stop the Book of Monsters. There was a giant explosion, and then Merlok—*poof*—disappeared. Thankfully, he managed to save a copy of himself inside the Knighton computer network. Now he's able to harness the power of magic and technology together."

"Got it," Fletch said, though he wasn't sure that he *totally* did. "Anyway, we're looking for a knight whose sword is pointed to the sky, right? I wonder if—"

Fletch wasn't able to finish his sentence.

He suddenly felt something: a sensation in his stomach, deep inside his belly. He swallowed hard. Sweat was quickly beginning to gather on his brow.

Not now, not now, not now, Fletch told himself.

For Fletch, this was not a new sensation. It had happened before, at the orphanage. He had come to call it *the feeling.*

The feeling seemed to happen at random moments, never predictable. Sometimes it was a passing sensation. Other times, it was mighty and overwhelming.

Fletch had not told a single living soul about *the feeling*. Never. He doubted he could even describe it if he tried. It was almost like a buzzing in his belly, or a hand gently pulling at his heart.

All people had gut feelings, sure—instincts—but this was different. It was *more* than instinct. *Beyond.*

Fletch's head began to feel light, and his legs seemed to be turning to rubber. He had to lean against a sculpture to catch his breath.

Never before had *the feeling* been this powerful.

"Are you okay?"

"Huh?" Fletch said.

Izzy was eyeing Fletch with a mixture of worry and curiosity. "Are you all right? You look, sort of, well, *not great.*"

Fletch had grown quite good at hiding *the feeling*. At the orphanage, when it hit him, he always managed to sneak away. He would often hide in the barn and wait for it to pass. *The feeling* embarrassed Fletch—it made him feel different from everyone else. And he never wanted that. Not at all. In fact, all Fletch had ever really wanted was to be like everyone else. Normal.

But he couldn't hide *the feeling* right now—no matter how hard he tried.

He looked at Izzy. His hands were trembling. "I'm fine," he said. "It's just this sensation. It happens sometimes. It's almost like, well, I don't know—"

Izzy cocked an eyebrow. "Go on," she encouraged. "Spit it out."

Fletch gulped. He did his best to steady his hands, and then decided—okay—he would try to explain. "It's like . . . Have you ever been someplace where you've never been before? But you don't feel lost? You feel like you know where to go, what street to walk down, what turn to take, or . . . I'm sorry, I'm not explaining it right."

Izzy scrunched up her eyes as she tried to understand. "You mean this feeling tells you where to go?"

"No. I mean, yes. I mean, only sometimes. Other times, it's like there's something there, at the edge of things. Just beyond my reach. Just outside my field of vision." Fletch lowered his head. "I know, I sound crazy. I'm weird. You picked the wrong partner. I'm sorry, Izzy."

Izzy chuckled. "Oh, shut up—weird is *good*. Who wants friends that are normal and regular?"

Fletch lifted his head. "Really?"

Izzy smiled warmly and nodded. "Okay, so . . . You're saying you've got some special, like, compass inside you. Correct?"

"Well, actually what—"

"We're following it," Izzy quickly said. "That's *what*."

"No, I've never . . ."

Izzy flashed a roguish grin. "It's time to remove 'never' from your vocab, Fletch. As of right now."

"But what about the field-quest?"

"You can't get into an adventure without breaking a few rules," Izzy said with a dismissive shrug. "You think Clay Moorington became the greatest knight in the land by always following the rules?"

"Actually, yes," Fletch said. "I heard he's Captain Rule Book, right?"

"Right, true, bad example. You know, I even heard Clay memorized the *entire* Knight's Code. He's, like, the most heroically heroic hero . . . ever. That's why he's the leader of the NEXO KNIGHTS team. And that's why he drives my brother so bonkers . . ."

"See!" Fletch said. "We should do what Clay would do! And Clay would finish the field-quest."

Izzy groaned. "But what about Macy? She's my *favorite* knight, and she only *became* a knight because she ignored her father. And he was the king! *Ignoring* what you're *supposed* to do can lead to *awesome stuff.* So what will it be, Fletch—the quest or *the feeling?*"

Fletch felt fear. Loads of it. But what was the point of fear? he thought. He had always been fearful. And like Izzy said, the Knights' Academy was a place where you could make your future and be who you wanted to be. Fletch liked the sound of that—a lot. And he *definitely* liked it more than the sound of "fear."

Finally, Fletch said, "*The feeling.* We follow *the feeling.*"

He didn't realize it at first, but he was then quickly walking down the hall. *The feeling* no longer felt so draining. Now that he had accepted it—he felt stronger, more confident, and no longer so frightened. *The feeling* was propelling him forward.

It was at that moment that the sculpture caught Fletch's attention. It snagged on something in his gut— something in *the feeling* made him pause. There was nothing special about this sculpture. It wasn't particularly interesting or strange—except for the fact *the feeling* was pushing him toward it.

He stopped beneath it.

Just then, they heard voices.

Izzy ducked around the side of the sculpture. Far, far down the hall, she caught a glimpse of Zilgo and Beak.

"If your gut is telling you to do something," said Izzy, "you need to do it quickly. The goon squad just arrived."

Fletch—not even sure why he was doing it—reached up and grabbed hold of the long iron lance that the sculpture's bronze hand clung to. Fletch figured he was breaking about a dozen academy rules right now, but it didn't stop him. He *yanked* on the lance.

CLICK.

The lance moved, shifting down.

The floor rumbled. The bronze base of the sculpture began to slowly slide backward, revealing a dark, round hole the size of a sewer entrance. Cool air rushed up from the blackness. Peering down the shaft, Fletch and Izzy saw the top rung of a ladder.

"What do you think?" Izzy asked.

Fletch looked at Izzy, an adventurous smile spreading across his face. "I think we just found a secret passageway."

Fletch knew this was no time to be hesitant: Zilgo and Beak were not far behind.

He swung his legs into the hole and began the climb down. Izzy quickly followed.

They had descended only a few feet when the metal ladder began to shudder. The sculpture was sliding back into place, and the dim light from the hall above was vanishing.

Nervously, Izzy said, "Fletch, did I mention I'm ever so slightly clumsy?"

"I sort of noticed."

"Well, if I slip and fall, it's on you. Literally."

Carefully, rung by rung, they climbed downward. The shaft was tight, and Fletch felt damp stone brushing against his shoulders. His hands became slick with sweat, and the darkness began to feel like a terrible blanket, enveloping him.

Fletch began to ponder all the worst-case scenarios—because that's how Fletch's mind worked. What if this ladder was a billion rungs long, and it went to the center of the earth? Or what if they were descending into some horrific monster-filled pit? Claustrophobic panic was overtaking *the feeling*.

And then, just as his hands became so sweaty he was sure he'd soon fall, his feet touched the ground.

"The catacombs!" Izzy said as she leapt down the remaining few rungs. "We're in the catacombs! I thought these were just a myth. It's a maze of old tunnels running beneath the city."

Fletch looked up at the ladder they had descended. It was tall. He guessed it was the height of two houses, at least. That meant they were *deep* beneath the academy now.

Happily, the catacombs were not as dark as the shaft had been. There was light: a dim blueness that seemed to radiate from all around them but at the same time from no place at all. It was like the air itself was shimmering.

Peering in the blueness, Fletch saw they were now in a long tunnel of cracked brick. It appeared to stretch on, endlessly, in either direction. Fletch thought back to earlier—how bright and wonderful and hopeful everything had felt as he entered the school for the first time. These dank catacombs felt like the mirror opposite: dark, foul, and uninviting.

"So," Izzy said, "this fancy smart gut of yours. Is it telling you left or right?"

Fletch checked his gut, examining *the feeling*, and then pointed right.

They began hiking the seemingly endless corridor. Fletch took careful steps at first, walking gingerly over the muddy ground. Soon they grew more confident and marched more quickly.

The tunnel snaked, curved, and zigzagged. The brick walls were crumbling and timeworn, and the ceiling dripped stale water. Heavy moisture hung in the air.

Squinting in the dim blue darkness, Fletch saw a fork in the tunnel, up ahead. A sudden realization came to him. "Izzy, if we go much farther, we'll *definitely* be off school grounds. Remember what Principal Brickland said? You could get kicked out. You've dreamed of being a knight, and if you get expelled . . ."

Izzy looked up at the gray brick ceiling, just a few feet above her head. "Fletch, I'm not sure if *below* school grounds counts as *off* school grounds."

"But that's just a technicality," Fletch said.

Izzy grinned. "Yeah, but *tech-nicalities* are my favorite *nicalities.*"

Suddenly, a gust of hot air came rushing down the corridor. It smelled like the inside of an old shoe. It was followed by an eerie echo—the sound of something alive.

KLIK-KLIK, KLIK-KLIK, KLIK-KLIK.

Fletch froze. Izzy's face was turning pale. She slowly glanced back down the corridor. "We can still go back, Fletch," she whispered.

Later on, Fletch would think of this moment often— and he would always be shocked by his response to Izzy. Because he *did* want to go back. There was a screaming in his brain, saying, *LEAVE! Get out of there, just go, turn and run, don't look back, don't stop. GO!*

But when Fletch opened his mouth, the words that came out were "I'm continuing ahead."

And Fletch meant it. He wasn't trying to sound brave

or appear heroic—he was *sure* he *would* do it. As sure as he'd ever been about anything. It was dark, the entire place felt haunted, and he risked becoming hopelessly and forever lost—but even without Izzy, he would press on.

He had ignored *the feeling* for his entire life.

But not anymore. He had to know where *the feeling* was leading him.

"You should go back, though," Fletch said to Izzy. "Really. I don't want you getting in trouble—or worse . . ."

Izzy took a deep breath and looked Fletch in the eyes. "Monstrox and his minions might be down here. Or some undiscovered villain! I can't let you go alone. It's *your* gut, it's *your* weird feeling—so it's *your* decision. But I'll follow you."

"Okay, let's—"

"But," Izzy said, flashing a teasing grin, "there better be something *really, really* rad at the end of all this."

With that, they marched on. The path wound and wound though endless twists and turns. At one point, Fletch was nearly certain they were walking in circles. Everything looked the same: the same grimy brick walls, the same murky-water-soaked ground, the same blue haze.

Bits of crumbled statues littered the path, cracking beneath their feet as they walked. Fletch saw cracked, ancient monster skulls embedded in the chipped tunnel walls. It felt like they were watching him.

"I wish I had a glow-torch," Izzy said. "Maybe we could see something."

And just as Izzy said that, she *did* see something. Izzy released a wild shriek and leapt about three feet into the air.

And Fletch saw why . . .

Crawling along the floor, just ahead, was a glowing blue creature. Inching closer, Fletch saw it was an enormous spider that appeared to be *mutated*. It looked like it was filled with electrical energy.

The spider paused, its fat hairy legs stabbed at the ground, and it turned to look back at Fletch and Izzy. It made a sound—the same sound they had heard earlier: *KLIK-KLIK, KLIK-KLIK, KLIK-KLIK.*

It quickly skittered ahead, darting around the corner.

Fletch glanced at Izzy. The blue light danced across her face—and he saw fear there. They didn't say a word, but they crept forward, turning the corner, following the beastly spider.

And they saw more.

Many more.

They saw spiders and snakes and bugs of all sizes. Insects and creepy-crawlies: all of them glowing blue.

Izzy threw a hand over her mouth to stop from shrieking. A short gasp escaped her mouth, barely audible over the chittering, clicking, and hissing of the creatures.

"Fletch," Izzy whispered, "I *really* hate to admit this, but bugs—man, oh, man—bugs *really freak me out.*"

For a moment, there was a proud gleam in Fletch's

eye. "Not me. Once you've seen a lobster the size of a bulldog, nothing grosses you out."

At once, the creatures all hurried down the hall—slithering, snaking, scurrying. Fletch and Izzy followed, and as they did, Fletch's feeling grew stronger.

"This way!" Fletch burst out, and began running. The muddy path splish-splashed and the blue light grew brighter. And as they rounded the corner, they both saw it at the same time and gasped.

A figure.

It stood at the very end of the corridor. Behind and around it, the passageway grew very wide. The figure was perfectly motionless. It glowed with energy: blue and silver.

Izzy quickly leapt up to the small ledge that ran along either side of the tunnel, and Fletch followed. They clung to the brick, concealing themselves in the shadowy gloom of the tunnel walls.

Izzy's voice was barely a whisper. "Is . . . is that a person up ahead?"

Fletch could hardly breathe, let alone speak. "I think."

Izzy peeked her head from out of the shadows, just long enough to steal a glance. "If it's a person," she said, "then it's the biggest person I've ever seen."

Fletch's heart pounded—but he forced his legs to

move, one foot in front of the next. "There's only one way to find out what it is, Izzy. Come on . . ."

The humming neon energy lit the way as Fletch and Izzy crept toward the strange figure. Sparks of electricity burst, and with every eruption, they saw more of the thing: a hood, two eyes, armor.

And then, one final burst—blindingly bright, like lightning—and it became clear . . .

"It's not a person at all!" Fletch realized.

"It's a statue!" Izzy exclaimed. "Made of stone."

Fletch brushed his hair from his eyes and realized he was slick with sweat. His heart was still thumping.

The blue energy was now so vivid that it illuminated the statue fully. A shimmering snake slithered around the statue's neck. It flashed a pair of venomous little black eyes and then disappeared over the stone shoulder. Fletch expected Izzy to flinch in fear, but she did not. Her fright had been replaced by curiosity.

"I think it's holding an upside-down shield," Izzy whispered.

But creeping even closer, they saw it wasn't a shield. Not *exactly.*

"It's a NEXO Power!" Izzy said. "Holy guacamole, we just discovered a new NEXO Power! At least, I *think* we did. Shields contain powers, and this looks like a shield, just upside down. Yep, I bet it's a *lost* NEXO Power. Buddy boy, they might just make you and I both knights *tomorrow*! We can skip the lame studying and cut straight to the monster fighting!"

But Fletch wasn't as sure as Izzy. A NEXO Power down here? Izzy knew much more about this stuff than he did, but it didn't seem to make sense. They were in a dead end, at the depths of the dark, dank catacombs. If it hadn't been for *the feeling*, they never would have found this place. It felt more like something someone *didn't* want to be found.

"C'mon, let's grab it!" Izzy said.

Fletch mumbled something and shook his head. He had a strange sense, certainly not the first one that day, but this one made his hair stand on an end. "Izzy," he said. "We should be careful."

Izzy dismissed his fears with a flick of her wrist. "Careful, shmareful."

Standing on her tippy-toes, she reached up, wrapping her hands around the shield. "See, nothing to worry—"

ZZZZZ-ZAP!

An earsplitting *KRAK!* exploded in the tight tunnel, hurling Izzy backward. She slammed into the catacomb wall, then splashed down onto her rear.

Fletch cried out, "Izzy!" and rushed toward her.

Her hair was frizzy and corkscrewed, and her eyes were practically spinning. "Whoa . . ." she said softly. "I feel like I just walked across the world's biggest carpet, barefoot, and then grabbed the world's metalest doorknob."

Fletch managed a relieved laugh. "You're okay?"

Izzy raised a shaky hand. "Little shocked, but all good."

Fletch stared up the shield that had just zapped his friend. And the longer he stared at it, the more peculiar he began to feel.

The feeling in his gut rose up into his chest. It was stretching, unfolding, and expanding inside him. His body grew warmer as *the feeling* spread, like hot apple cider flowing through him from head to toe.

It no longer felt like he was even inside his own body. It was like he was someone else, some other person, *watching Fletch*. Like he was inside a dream.

The shield was growing in size, filling his vision.

It felt like soda bubbles were dancing on the surface of his hands. There, Fletch felt the energy most.

It took him a moment to realize that his hands were *moving*. They were darting and dancing through the air, like he was conducting an orchestra. They moved slowly at first, then quicker and quicker.

Izzy spoke, but the words sounded distant and faint. It reminded Fletch of being back in the orphanage, when the headmaster would call him to supper, but he was two floors up, behind a closed door.

Colors appeared. They came from Fletch's hands. Swirling shades, trailing through the air—like he was painting, but there was no canvas and he held no brush.

The bright, brilliant colors snapped Fletch back to the present. He heard Izzy clearly now, asking over and over, "Fletch, *what is happening*?!"

"I don't know!" Fletch cried out.

His hands continued slicing and cutting through the air. Following each movement were vividly intense reds, whites, green, blues, and yellows.

And then—suddenly—the colors disappeared. But they were replaced with something even stranger . . . Without warning, white-hot bolts of lightning leapt from Fletch's hands! The electricity shot into the statue, linking Fletch to the strange stone figure.

Slowly—almost imperceptibly—the statue *moved*.

The electricity swirled around the statue, and the statue's arms stirred. Bits of pebble crumbled and ages-old dust filled the air. The statue seemed to be awakening from a very long, very deep slumber.

"Get back!" Izzy shouted. "It's coming to life!"

But Fletch simply stared in fascinated fright. Bolts

of lightning continued to erupt from his hands. Izzy grabbed him, trying to tug him away. But she couldn't move him—not until the energy eruption slowed and the lightning assault ended. Whatever strange, enchanted act Fletch had been performing—it was now complete.

The statue's giant stone hands extended. It held out the shield. It was *giving* it to Fletch . . .

CHAPTER FOUR

Elsewhere in the kingdom of Knighton . . .

A tired, ancient knight sat on a throne of bone inside a crumbling mansion. The knight had been sleeping. He slept often, and he woke rarely. But something now caused him to stir. He sensed an awakening.

The knight's ancient hand was all bone. The skeletal hand raised and then came smashing down on the arm of his throne.

The bony bang caused six more knights to rise. These knights had been sleeping on the floor of the crumbling mansion's throne room. They were smaller than the tired, ancient knight, and they wore very little armor. They were skeletons: walking, speaking, living skeletons.

"Sir B, you're awake?" one skeletal knight asked nervously.

The tired, ancient knight—Baron von Bludgeonous—spoke. His voice was a growl, dry and harsh. "A power has been found. A Rogul has woken. I sense it."

The skeletal knights shuffled forward. "Should we retrieve it?" one asked.

"Of *course* you should retrieve it!" Baron von Bludgeonous barked.

The same knight said, "Okay, sure, great. I wasn't sure if maybe we should hang around, run you a bath or something, cook up some nachos, and then retrieve the Power later, or—"

"You *twerp!*" Baron von Bludgeonous barked. "You are my knights! I am your liege! You do as I command! And you do it *immediately*. The nachos can wait . . ."

The skeletal knight quickly nodded. As he did, the weight of his helmet almost caused his bony neck to crack and his entire cranium to tumble straight off. He caught his head an instant before it fell.

Baron von Bludgeonous rose, lifted a lance nearly as large as he was, and jabbed it forward. "Go! To the catacombs! *NOW!*"

"Dude, what *was* all that?" Izzy exclaimed, practically hopping from foot to foot. "Wait, don't answer. I'll tell you what that was. That was *the single coolest thing I've ever seen!*"

Fletch had no words for Izzy. He felt only his own fading adrenaline and a mixture of shock, surprise, and excitement.

"We should probably take that," Izzy said, nodding toward the upside-down shield. "You know, don't look a gift statue in the mouth and all. But how?"

Fletch stared at the extended shield with narrow-eyed determination—then he reached for it. Izzy's eyes opened wide, but some strange instinct told Fletch he would not get zapped.

As he reached for it, the shield began to glow even brighter. It was like the energy had retreated from the statue and the ground and the walls and the air and was now contained entirely *within* the shield.

Fletch wrapped both arms around it, like he was giving it a great big hug, and pulled it from the statue's hands.

Fletch slowly turned. "I got it . . ." he said softly.

Then Fletch saw Izzy's face turn ghostly white. "F-F-Fletch . . ." she stuttered. "Behind you."

Fletch heard it before he saw it. The base of the statue was crumbling and breaking apart, revealing a vortex of blue energy. Stones swirled, trapped in the tornado of electricity. The statue looked different now—still stone, but *alive.*

Fletch staggered back.

"We should maybe run now . . ." Izzy said.

They did—and the statue followed. Fletch and Izzy raced down the long corridor. Behind them, the statue moved like a shark, swimming through the air.

"Maybe we should give the shield back!" Fletch cried out. "It's not ours!"

"It's a NEXO Power! We can't give it back. Merlok needs to know about this!"

The shield was as tall as they were and almost as wide. It wasn't particularly heavy, but it also wasn't easy to run with, and Fletch was soon gasping for breath. Izzy led the way, retracing their steps, trying to recall the winding path they had taken.

Suddenly, Fletch slid to a stop. "Listen!"

Izzy glanced behind her. The statue hovered and zoomed down the corridor, closing in. "No stopping! No listening! That weird statue isn't far behind! It might eat us."

Fletch frowned. "You think a statue is going to eat us?"

"I don't know! I've never encountered a living statue before! Eat us, beat us, pummel us, pulverize us—who knows?"

Fletch lifted his hand to his mouth. He heard hollow, light footsteps, and the rattling of loose armor. A moment later, the clattering of metal and bone echoed through the corridor as six skeletal knights rounded the corner. Fletch and Izzy gasped as the undead fiends charged toward them, clad in rusty armor and waving rusty swords.

Fletch and Izzy were trapped, helplessly stuck in the narrow tunnel, with skeletons racing from one direction and the monstrous statue zooming in from the other. And as the statue charged, it drew back a heavy, glowing, energy-filled hand.

The statue's thick stone hand flung forward!

Fletch and Izzy prepared for the worst—to be struck by this giant, come-to-life statue. But instead, the stone hand passed between their faces . . .

Fletch's eyes popped as he watched it slam into the closest skeletal knight. The knight exploded, instantly reduced to a scattered pile of bone and armor.

"It punched that skeleton guy, not us!" Izzy exclaimed with relief. "By the way, Fletch, *there are skeleton guys here!*"

A second knight drew back his sword. "A Rogul is

present!" he growled to the others. "The power has been discovered!"

Fletch and Izzy exchanged looks of mutual confusion and weirded-out-ness. "A Rogul?"

The statue—which was apparently called a Rogul—continued forward. Izzy darted to the side, allowing the Rogul to float past. "I'm here to help!" she said as she grabbed the bottom of the shield, helping Fletch hold it.

The Rogul scooped up the first knight and flung him into the wall. Another knight slipped past, forcing Fletch and Izzy to quickly backpedal.

"Hello, children," the approaching skeletal knight said, lifting his sword. The corroded metal of the blade shined an eerie, dancing line on his gray-white skull. "That power does not belong to you."

Fletch and Izzy took careful steps backward. "Izzy," Fletch said. "I'm starting to think we never should have left the academy . . ."

"It was your feeling we followed!" Izzy exclaimed.

"Well, now I'm feeling like it was a mistake!" Fletch shot back.

"Is it your fancy gut telling you that, or is it the small undead army?"

"Bit of both."

"Lift!" Izzy cried.

KLASH!

The knight's sword came crashing down. Fletch and Izzy—each gipping one side of the shield—raised it high, blocking the blow. The knight continued, jabbing the blade into the shield, pushing Fletch and Izzy back, back, back. The steel sparked in the darkness.

The skeletal knight's blank, dull eye sockets were alight with something like fury. But before he could strike again—

SNATCH!

The Rogul scooped the knight into the air. A roar came from the Rogul's mouth—a totally lame, totally squeaky roar. It sounded like a burping kitten. With a single squeeze, the Rogul's heavy hand broke the knight into pieces.

And then the Rogul zoomed toward the remaining knights, quickly crushing a trio of the bone bad guys.

KRUNCH!

KRAK!

BURST!

Only one knight remained. His eyeholes popped wide, and he quickly dropped his sword. "Baron von Bludgeonous will hear of this! And he'll be mad! Real, real mad!" the knight shouted, then quickly turned and fled, disappearing into the shadowy darkness. Apparently, he had had enough Rogul for one day.

Izzy glanced at the scattered bones and the hovering Rogul. "Uh, now what?" she asked.

"Now we get back to the academy," Fletch said. He grunted and used both hands to hoist the shield. "We'll move quicker if one of us carries this."

An instant later, Fletch *seriously* regretted offering to carry the shield. His back ached like he'd spent three straight days on the salt farm.

"And what about this dude?" Izzy asked. "The Rogul."

Fletch eyed the come-to-life statue. "Maybe now we'll just sort of go our separate ways?" he said hopefully.

But they did not go their separate ways.

And unfortunately, getting back to the Knights' Academy was easier said than done. Fletch and Izzy spent nearly two hours wandering the catacombs, and the Rogul followed the entire way.

Fletch and Izzy tried everything to get the strange, magical statue to leave: yelling, hiding, distracting, commanding, fleeing—but none of it worked. When they finally found the ladder again, the Rogul was still with them—and Fletch saw they had a second problem.

Peering up the dark shaft, and then down at the shield, Fletch realized he had *zero idea* how to both climb *and* carry the thing. He sighed. "So now what?" he asked Izzy. "How do we get back with the shield?"

"Question," Izzy said, "is it a shield? Or a NEXO Power? What are we calling it? It *looks* like a shield, but it *is* a NEXO Power."

"What it *is*," Fletch said, "is *heavy enough* that neither of us can get it up a two-story ladder."

With that, Fletch let the shield drop to the damp floor. He leaned against the wall, catching his breath. What a day, he thought. What an *afternoon*. He looked at Izzy, and she seemed to be thinking the same thing— because they both began giggling. A moment later, they were both howling with laughter. As they waited, trying to figure out how they would get the shield (or was it a power?) up the ladder, it hit them all at once: the adventure, the battling, the skeletal knights, the statue. Fletch had expected the first day of Knight Academy to be overwhelming—but this was simply *beyond*.

"HA. HA. HA."

And then the Rogul was laughing—a slow, hard, heavy snorting sound.

"So he's got a sense of humor?" Izzy asked. "This just keeps getting better . . ."

Fletch brushed his hair from his eyes as he

contemplated a plan. "Hey, you think he wants to do us a favor?"

The Rogul, somehow, seemed to understand what Fletch was hinting at. The statue bent over—a very strange-looking action—and lifted the shield. That was it! *That* was how they'd get the power to the top of the ladder!

No more laughing, just climbing.

Fletch gabbed the rungs, and Izzy followed. Glancing back, Fletch happily saw that he was correct: The Rogul followed. It climbed with them, though it didn't seem to need to actually *climb*—its swirling lower body simply pushed it upward.

Fletch was pondering how they would move the sculpture so they could reenter the academy, when the shaft rumbled and shook—the same as when they entered. He realized that the ladder rung he was gripping was actually a switch. The switch had closed the secret passage earlier, and now it was opening it.

Fletch hoisted himself up, Izzy followed, and the Rogul came up last. Coming up into the Hall of Knights, Fletch was relieved to see there was no one around. Izzy removed her glasses and blinked as her eyes readjusted to the warm glow of the academy.

The Rogul thrust out his arms, extending the shield. Slipping her glasses back on, Izzy eagerly reached for it—but the Rogul quickly yanked the shield away. Fletch then tried, and the Rogul instantly handed it over.

"I think he likes you better," Izzy said. "Good punching skills, terrible judge of character."

"I guess so," Fletch said, then added, "Hey, do you hear that?"

A commotion was drifting in from a window near the exit. Izzy was suddenly sprinting the length of the hall.

Fletch glanced at the Rogul. "She's kind of overeager."

"*GRUNT.*"

"Come look!" Izzy hollered. "It's that rat Zilgo! He and Beak found Ned Knightley's Silver Sword of Silverness."

Fletch hurried over, and the Rogul hovered behind him. At the window, Fletch saw the first-year students gathered on the training grounds far below. Principal Brickland was—reluctantly, it appeared, and with some annoyance—congratulating Zilgo and Beak on winning the field-quest.

Fletch and Izzy both let out similarly frustrated groans. "It should have been ours," Fletch said. "Zilgo just bribed and cheated his way to the prize. He followed us, and from there it was probably a cinch."

Izzy's frown suddenly flipped, and she waved a dismissive hand. "Pshht. Who wants a dusty old sword? We got something much better—a NEXO Power!"

Fletch gulped as an unsettling question entered his mind: What would they do with the power? They couldn't just bring it to Principal Brickland or Merlok. They would know they had left academy grounds. And it would require so much explaining—explaining of things Fletch wasn't ready to explain. Like *the feeling*.

Sharing that with Izzy had been hard enough, but sharing it with the principal? And then, probably, with the whole academy? Everyone finding out? Students, teachers, Squirebots—*everyone*. The very thought made him want to curl up in a ball beneath a blanket and never, well, *uncurl*.

"Izzy, we can't just hand over the power. We can't. I can't."

"I know. We'll figure something out. But first, more important, we need to stash this guy," Izzy said, waving a hand toward the Rogul. "Quickly, while everyone's outside."

Fletch eyed the huge, hovering statue. "Where can we *possibly* hide him?"

Izzy grinned.

"What? Why are you smiling like that?"

Izzy grinned even bigger, and her eyes twinkled—and then Fletch knew. And Fletch just groaned . . .

The residential halls were halfway across campus, but Izzy knew a series of shortcuts. They avoided the main halls and stairwells, and thus avoided being spotted creeping across campus with a massive living statue—which was good, because Fletch was certain that was a no-no.

Entering the long first-year dormitory halls, Fletch quickly spotted his ratty, beat-up traveling bag resting against a door. It had been delivered, just like Principal Brickland said. Hoisting it over his shoulder, Fletch said, "I guess this is my dorm."

Fletch and Izzy carried the shield into the dorm room, and the Rogul quickly hovered in behind her. "Sure, sure," Fletch muttered. "Everyone's welcome."

With the door shut, he turned to Izzy. "I've made up my mind. *I'll* bring the NEXO Power to Principal Brickland. I'll say I went alone. I won't mention *the feeling* or the skeletons or anything. I won't mention you, Izzy. You shouldn't get in trouble just because of my gut."

Izzy shook her head. "Nice try, buddy boy, but I'm getting credit, too. Maybe we should ask my brother what to do?"

"Do you trust him?"

"He's my brother!"

"So do you trust him?" Fletch asked.

"Actually no, not really," Izzy said with a sigh.

They heard a commotion from the hall—first-year students returning from the field-quest. The students were finding their bags, finding their dorms. Zilgo's voice boomed, loudly boasting about his win.

"I should get to my room," Izzy said as she opened the door and stepped into the hall. "I'll come get you in a bit, for dinner."

"You're *really* just leaving this Rogul guy here?" Fletch said.

Izzy looked up at the hovering statue. "You're the one he likes," she said with a grin. "Look at that, first day of school, and you made *two* friends."

Fletch rolled his eyes—although, inside, that observation *did* make him feel good.

Izzy was about to shut the door, when she stopped and glanced back at her friend. "Hey, Fletch, one last thing that we didn't have time to chat about."

Fletch cocked an eyebrow.

Izzy beamed with excitement. "Buddy, *you have magic powers.*"

CHAPTER FIVE

Meanwhile, at the crumbling old mansion . . .

Baron von Bludgeonous was displeased. *Most displeased.* He announced his displeasure by lifting his lance and slamming it, over and over, into his bone throne. Bits and pieces of the skeletal structure splintered and cracked.

Baron von Bludgeonous stopped—catching his undead, lungless breath—and turned to the knight that had delivered the bad news. The skeletal knight was so nervous he was shaking. His trembling bones rattled with a loud, clackety-clackety sound.

In a dry, sand-sucking voice, Baron von Bludgeonous said, "Explain what happened. Now."

"We found the power, Your Liegeness," the skeletal knight said.

"It's *my* liege," Baron von Bludgeonous said, correcting the knight. "Or *Your* Highness. Not *Your Liegeness.*"

"My Highness?" the knight asked.

Baron von Bludgeonous sighed—a raspy sound—and lifted the lance, ready to thwomp his bony minion. "It's 'my liege' or 'Your Highness'—one or the other! But you don't mix the 'yours' and the 'mys'! Can you understand that? Are you capable?"

The trembling knight stammered. "I understand, my high—um . . . *Your* Highness. Like I was saying, we found the power—but it had been already removed from the Rogul."

Baron von Bludgeonous' bony eyelids formed a half-curious, half-furious V shape. "Removed?"

"Yes. Taken by two children."

"Children? Are you positive they were not, say, very, very, very tiny adults?"

"No, they were most certainly children. They mentioned the academy. One was a boy, and the Rogul seemed to be protecting him."

"How interesting . . ." Baron von Bludgeonous said, an eerie smile forming.

The stammering knight continued. "But it was the Rogul that started punching us. Or no, *pummeling*! *Yes*, yes, pummeling us! He turned the other knights to nothing but piles of bone!"

"But you?" Baron von Bludgeonous said to the knight. "You are *not* a pile of bone?"

"N-no. I'm still standing."

"Do not fail me again," Baron von Bludgeonous said. "Or you *will* be a pile of bone. A small, timid, *useless* pile of bone. Understand?"

"I think so . . ." the knight said. "You mean, you'll hit me with your lance, right?"

Baron von Bludgeonous sighed, sank into his bone throne, and massaged his bony temples. "Yes," he muttered. "That's what I meant . . ."

"What about the knights that were left behind?"

"I will raise them again, as always," Baron von Bludgeonous said. "Crumble them. Crush them. No matter—they are already dead. I can always bring them back. Like Monstrox, who conjures monsters as he pleases."

Baron von Bludgeonous dismissed the knight with a flick of his wrist bone. As the knight retreated to the depths of the mansion, Baron von Bludgeonous tapped the bony armrest while his warped mind processed the strange information.

A boy, Baron von Bludgeonous thought. *A boy was able to remove a power from a Rogul. And now the Rogul has, as always, become the defender of the one who freed him.*

Baron von Bludgeonous was impressed.

"Whoever this boy is," he said aloud, to no one but the empty room, "he must possess great power. And thus, I must destroy him."

"What are you?" Fletch asked.

The Rogul did not respond.

Chitchat seemed to be out of the question, so Fletch took in his dormitory room. He had never had his own room before, ever, so he was excited, even though the room was simple, plain, and nearly empty. There was a bed, a nightstand, a closet, a desk—and not much else.

With some work, Fletch had managed to shove the power beneath his bed. With that bit of business done, he again set about trying to communicate with the Rogul. And still, it wasn't going well . . .

"What. Are. You?" Fletch asked.

"GRUNT."

Fletch sighed and swept the hair from his eyes. He had never been so confused in his *life*. His head was spinning.

Fletch imagined one of the orphans, back home, asking him about the Knights' Academy. "How was your first day?" they'd want to know.

And Fletch would reply, "Oh you know, a totally normal first day—except that I discovered I have some strange and tremendously powerful power and I awakened a stone statue monster and that stone statue monster saved me and my friend. I have a new friend now, by the way, I think—at least for now—and she's sort of famous, but yeah, anyway, the stone statue monster *rescued* us from a band of skeletal undead knights

after we discovered a long-lost NEXO Power. So yeah, totally normal first day."

Fletch sunk down onto his bed, and his thoughts were quickly replaced by a wonderful sensation beneath his rear end. He had heard that other students complained that academy beds were uncomfortable— but Fletch realized those other students must have been sleeping in some *fancy* beds previously, because this thing was crazy comfy. Maybe it was because he had just had the longest—but also most fly-by-fastest!—day of his life, but he thought it was the coziest thing he had ever sat on.

He wanted to rest. He wondered if maybe he'd wake up and discover that this had all been one wickedly weird dream?

"*GRUNT.*"

Sigh. The Rogul. Of course, the Rogul. The strange living statue that he was hiding in his room. This was no dream . . .

"Do you need, like, a drink or anything?" Fletch asked.

"*GRUNT.*"

"Right. Grunt. Well, what about food?"

"*GRUNT.*"

"You're not going to, like, crush me in my sleep tonight are you?"

"*GRUNT.*"

"I'm hoping that's a no . . . ?"

"*GRUNT.*"

"I need to unpack my bags. Well, bag—singular. I need to brush my teeth. And I need to—" Fletch was interrupted by a gaping, practically jaw-shattering yawn.

In response, the Rogul yawned—or at least, the Rogul *imitated* a yawn. Fletch chuckled. "You get sleepy?"

"*GRUNT.*"

"Okay, good answers. Solid chat. Look, I'm *beyond tired.* I'm going to lie down on the bed and shut my eyes before dinner. But *just* for five minutes. Maybe ten. Fifteen minutes, tops—definitely no more than twenty minutes. Do me a favor, Rogul—wake me up after twenty-five minutes, okay?"

"*GRUNT.*"

Right. Fletch lay back and let his body sink into the bed. His head hit the straw-stuffed pillow, and he was asleep in seconds . . .

Fletch was awakened—but not by the Rogul.

He was awakened first by the sun, beaming through his second-story window like a yellow-orange spotlight.

That caused him to blink.

And then the sound of clashing and clanging outside: battle practice.

That caused him to sit up.

And then a loud rapping at his door. *KNOCK! KNOCK! KNOCK!*

That caused him to spring out of bed. His eyes shot to the alarm clock on the dresser—one of the few things in the room that the academy provided.

"Oh no! Eight o'clock in the morning!" Fletch exclaimed.

The Rogul hovered exactly where it had hovered twelve hours earlier. The statue hadn't moved an inch, which, Fletch supposed, made sense—it was a statue, after all.

"You were supposed to get me up after twenty-five minutes!" Fletch shouted, his voice an anxious shriek.

"GRUNT."

KNOCK! KNOCK! KNOCK!

"Argh, too many sounds!" Fletch groaned. He hurried to the door and cracked it open, wary of someone catching a glimpse of the Rogul. But as soon as Fletch inched open the door, it swung open fully, and Izzy hurried inside.

"Morning, morning, buddy boy!" Izzy said, smiling cheerfully. She was like a walking, talking energy drink. "You slept through dinner last night. But you didn't miss much, just a few duds fawning over Zilgo. They put Ned Knightley's Silver Sword of Silverness on a big pedestal in the Hall of Knights. Zilgo wouldn't shut up about it."

"Great . . ." Fletch said.

"You missed breakfast, too. And if you don't get moving, you'll *also* miss our first class."

Fletch groaned. His stomach did the same. "I haven't eaten in forever."

Izzy thrust a paper bag into Fletch's hand. "I brought you sausages and donuts. What are buds for? Now move it or lose it, Fletch my friend. I'll be outside. Be speedy, huh?"

Not more than four minutes later, Fletch had devoured three donuts and two greasy sausage links, showered, dressed, brushed his teeth, and ran a hand over his hair.

Again, he inched open the door—and this time he yanked Izzy into his dormitory. "What are we supposed to do about *him*?" Fletch asked, waving at the Rogul.

Izzy shrugged. "Leave him here. Let him hang."

"I can't *let him hang*," Fletch said. "Look, he follows me. I discovered that not-so-great feature when I stepped out of the shower and the Rogul was just floating there, in the bathroom."

"Sounds like it was weird," Izzy said.

"It was."

"Wait. What exactly do you mean, 'follows'?" Izzy asked.

"Like every single step!" Fletch said. He demonstrated: walking to the far corner of the room, the Rogul floating along, just behind him.

"No biggie. We'll just lock the door behind us," Izzy said.

"What if someone comes in?" Fletch cried. "I don't know how the academy works. Maybe they do a dorm check or something."

Izzy whistled quietly, thinking, while she glanced around the room. "When my mom used to make me clean my room, I'd just shove everything in the closet . . ."

There was one closet. Izzy flung open the door, and together, she and Fletch managed to squeeze the Rogul inside. Fletch threw his bag up the top shelf, and then they shut the door. An instant later, the Rogul was bumping into the door, attempting to leave.

BUMP.

BUMP.

BUMP.

Izzy frowned for a moment, then said with perky positivity, "Don't fret. He'll tire himself out. Now— *COME ON!*"

"I gotta make my bed!" Fletch said.

"What for? Why make your bed? It's just gonna get mussed again."

"I make my bed every day! Otherwise, you don't get dinner."

Izzy rolled her eyes. "Fletch, you're not at the sad deep-woods orphanage anymore. Let's *gooooo!*"

Fletch glanced back at the closet door. He wasn't convinced the Rogul would just tire himself out . . .

BUMP.

BUMP.

BUMP.

Fletch quickly yanked the sheet off his bed, looped the whole thing through the closet door handles, and knotted it shut. "Sorry, Rogul," Fletch said. "But I'll be back! Promise!"

And with that, he followed Izzy out into the hall. School was under way . . .

CHAPTER SIX

"Take after your brother, I see? No respect for rules, no respect for schedules, no respect for *other people's time.*"

Izzy and Fletch exchanged worried glances. It was their first class: Combat Skills. And they had just come in late.

Captain Clash was tall and thin, and his face reminded Fletch of horse leather. There was a long scar on his face, running from his eye to his throat. He had a face that made Fletch think of great battles, fought long ago. He seemed like a man from another time.

Captain Clash towered over Izzy. "You're a Richmond," he said. "That might mean something to some of these kids—but it means *zero* to me. Monstrox doesn't care that you're a Richmond. A Grimroc won't care that you're a Richmond when it's swinging a battle-axe at your golden-haired head. You understand?"

"Yes," Izzy said quietly.

"Yes . . . ?"

"Yes, *Captain Clash*," Izzy said.

"Good. Take your seats."

"Sure. And *where* would you like us to take them?" Izzy asked, flashing a jokey grin. Captain Clash did not laugh. Fletch did not laugh. No one laughed. Izzy hung her head, swallowed, and quickly followed Fletch to the nearest bench.

Fletch glanced around, taking in the marvelous high-tech classroom. Huge shelves stacked with books loomed over the students. The walls were covered with images of knights in full combat armor. Globes and maps and glowing monitors filled the room. A huge window ran the length of the room, offering a view of the towering Knightonia skyline. Fletch could hardly believe that this was his new home—that this was where he'd be spending his days, learning.

Captain Clash wasted no time getting down to

business—class had barely begun, and he was already defining and discussing battle tactics. The only things Fletch *ever* battled were crabs, cod, and the occasional axfish—and that was just trying to get them in the boat. He had swung an axe to chop boulders, but he was terrible at it. He had chased field mice out of the kitchen with a broom. But that was the full extent of his battle experience. Oh, and in the catacombs, where he had blocked, bobbed, and backpedaled. Basically everything possible to *avoid* fighting those skeletal—

Fletch felt a sharp jab at his side. "Huh?"

Izzy shot him a look. Fletch saw that Captain Clash was leaning over the desk, staring with eyes that seemed to jolt straight through him.

"Trouble hearing, Mr. Bowman?" the professor asked.

"No, sir," Fletch said. "At least, not that I know of. Y'know, I never had a proper hearing test. So I guess I *could* have trouble hearing. Makes you wonder . . ." Fletch said, and he immediately began to ponder the range and effectiveness of his hearing.

Izzy quickly shot an elbow into her friend's side and whispered, *"Just answer the question!"*

"Oh. Right. Sorry. I hear fine. Could you just, I apologize, repeat the question, Captain Clash?"

Captain Clash sighed. "I said, as a knight, what manner of weapon do you plan on wielding?"

Fletch felt his eyebrows furrow. His mind raced about. Then he simply admitted the truth: He had no idea, and he hadn't given it any thought.

A quick gasp filled the classroom. And then silence. And then laughter. Fletch glanced back at the other students—they were looking at him like he had tentacles sprouting from his head. Even Izzy groaned.

A voice from the back called out, "Never given a thought to his weapon! He'd make a better Knights' Academy *janitor* than an actual knight!"

Of course, it was Zilgo, chuckling wildly with Beak and a few other first-year boys. Fletch felt hot. If only Zilgo knew that he, Fletch, was different than *any* of them—that Fletch had powers they could never comprehend! Powers that even *he* couldn't understand!

"Problem with janitors, Ethan?" another voice asked. "Did you know my father was the maintenance man at the king's castle?"

Fletch glanced back. The voice belonged to an older student, who was in the rear of the room, leaning against a bookshelf. This student had shaggy brown hair like Fletch's, and sharp, pointed eyebrows.

"That's Robin Underwood," Izzy whispered. "He's a second-year student. He helps Merlok 2.0 with top secret projects—*so cool!*"

Captain Clash announced Robin as a year-two apprentice and teacher's assistant. He explained that Robin would be helping throughout the year—and that today, he'd be leading the class.

Robin quickly bounded up the steps to the teacher's stage and tapped a long blue monitor that nearly ran the length of the room. An image of an armor suit appeared—and the entire class sat up, eager.

Robin said, "Every knight needs a metal suit of armor to protect them. This armor is the ultimate in high-tech—but it only reaches full strength when a NEXO Power is used. The NEXO Power shoots through the armor, giving knights extra strength, skills, and protection."

Another image appeared on the large screen: a shield. Robin continued. "A knight's shield is one of their most important possessions. NEXO KNIGHT shields are like traditional shields—only *way* better. The face of each shield is a Wi-Fi interface and a digital screen. Merlok can deliver NEXO Powers to the knights via their shields. All a knight has to do is hold up their shield and call out 'Merlok . . . NEXOOOOO KNIGHT!' Then a beam shoots up in the air from the shield and links with Merlok 2.0. Next, the NEXO Powers transfer in. Boom! That easy."

Looking at the shield on-screen, Fletch realized Izzy was right: It *did* look like the one they had found in the catacombs. But at the same time, it *didn't*. Something about it seemed different. The more Fletch thought about it, the more he felt they should *definitely* just go tell Principal Brickland what they'd found.

"Sound fun?" Robin asked the class.

Izzy thought it did—she was shaking with excitement. The whole table was jumping.

Robin revealed a taunting, playful smirk. "Well, guess what—you guys don't get your armor or your shields yet. A shield is only given to graduating knights after they have completed their education at the Knights' Academy. It is a badge of excellence, honor, and pride. So yeah ... not yet! You'll start with the Novix system—it's the training version for knights-to-be. Basically, NEXO Powers for beginners."

A disappointed groan filled the room.

"Don't worry. You'll have a blast," Robin said as he strode toward the Novix machine. It was a large device, about the size of a refrigerator, covered in knobs and switches and blinking lights. It glowed with the same blue light that filled much of the academy.

Robin tapped the machine. "This Novix machine sends simulated NEXO Powers to your first-year training shields. Get it? Got it? Good."

With that, Captain Clash tapped a button, and panels on the walls flew open. Suits of training armor appeared—sliding out, like they were on coat hangers. The students jumped to their feet, and an amazed gasp filled the room. On another wall, a panel emerged to reveal an array of weapons: swords and daggers and maces and lances.

Captain Clash waved at the armory. "Robin, I'll let you take it from here this morning."

"Suit up!" Robin announced.

"Oh man, this is *great*!" Izzy said.

Izzy grinned and followed the other students. They all hurried to the racks, eager to slip into their gear. It took Fletch nearly ten minutes to get into his armor. He only had the chest plate on, and the other students were already finished. Fletch managed to get into one boot but then tripped, stumbled into the wall, and was pretty sure he almost broke his nose. Not a great start. Izzy hurried over and helped him finish.

"She help you put your underwear on, too?" Zilgo asked with a snicker.

Robin walked the classroom, showing the other students small tricks—flipping toggles and tightening gauntlets.

Next was the question of weaponry—the question that had earlier caused the whole class to regard Fletch as some sort of daft fool.

Gesturing to the armory wall, Robin directed the students to choose a weapon. "Try them out, feel the weight, find something you're comfortable with."

The students dashed toward the weapons like they were birthday presents, waiting to be opened.

Fletch took a few steps forward, then a few back. By the time he actually *made* it to the big Wall o' Weapons, only one item remained: a bow and arrow.

What am I supposed to do with that? Fletch thought.

All around the room, students were experimenting with their new weapons. Swords were swung, and spears were thrust. Izzy had chosen a mace covered in short spikes—and she already wielded it like a pro. Fletch watched, jealous.

"Stuck with the ol' bow and arrow, huh?" a friendly voice said.

Fletch looked up to see Robin. Fletch shrugged—and immediately realized how hard it was to shrug while wearing forty pounds of armor. "Guess so."

Robin smiled warmly. "Aaron Fox uses a bow, too, and he might be the most radical knight there is."

For a moment, Fletch felt better about the high-tech blue bow in his hands.

"We'll end your first combat class with some quick sparring," Robin announced. "Light contact. No real damage. Partner up, gang!"

Oh, come on! Partnering up—again!? Fletch thought. At least this time, he knew Izzy would be his—

"I'll take Fletch!" Zilgo barked. The boy's eyes danced with mischievous delight. Fletch scowled.

The students spaced out, and the sparring was soon under way. The room was filled with clanging and banging. Fletch had hoped to observe, just for a moment—but Zilgo quickly stomped toward an open space in the corner. "Here. Now."

Fletch's shoulders sagged as he reluctantly followed. He glanced down at his bow and arrow. He might as well have been holding a feather duster . . .

"Hey, Fletch," Zilgo said. "Sorry about the jokes before. I didn't mean that stuff."

Fletch glared.

"I'm serious," Zilgo said. He stuck out a hand. "Fair fight? Friends?"

Fletch grudgingly stuck out his hand. "Fine, I guess we can—"

In a flash, Zilgo yanked on Fletch's hand, throwing him into the wall! Zilgo swung his blade. Fletch managed to duck and lift his shoulder, just barely blocking the blow. The sword clanged against Fletch's armor.

Furious, Fletch forgot all about his bow and arrow—and instead charged Zilgo. He was going to tackle him, pummel him, anything he could. But Zilgo quickly spun, thrusting out a foot, causing Fletch to trip and crash to the floor.

As he scrambled to his feet, Zilgo slammed the hilt of his blade into Fletch's chest plate. The blow knocked the wind from Fletch's lungs. He flung his helmet off and buckled over, gasping for air.

"Zilgo!"

The bully turned—just as Izzy swung! There was a deafening CLANK as Zilgo was taken clean off his feet.

"Why don't you fight someone with a little training?" Izzy said.

The other students all lowered their weapons. They gathered, eager to watch Izzy duel Zilgo.

"Bring it," Zilgo snarled.

Izzy stepped back, gripped her weapon, and charged!

Izzy raced toward Zilgo. Zilgo sped toward Izzy. Each had their weapons raised, ready to strike. But just then—

Captain Clash leapt between them! He thrust out his armored hands and—*CLANG!*—Izzy's club was knocked from her hands and Zilgo's sword clattered to the floor. "Enough!" Captain Clash barked.

"Robin Underwood," the captain said, turning to face the second-year student. "Were you simply going to allow these two first-year students to bash each other?"

Robin shrugged. "Totally not. Was just going to let them go at it long enough to see how much Izzy learned from her big bro."

Captain Clash simply glared . . .

When the trumpet sounded and class was over, Fletch didn't think he'd ever been so happy and relieved in his life. But his happiness was short-lived.

Captain Clash made a final announcement. "All students will battle tomorrow in our first-year combat competition, known as . . . the *Combatition*. It allows me to judge your abilities and group you by skill level. So rest up!"

Fletch sighed as he and Izzy they made their way down the hall to their next class. "We have to go back there *again*? To fight, *again*?"

Izzy grinned eagerly. "Nope, even better! Tomorrow, we fight in the Academy Arena!"

"Academy Arena?" Fletch asked.

"Yup, it's *sick*. It's this huge structure that comes out of the ground! The grass slides apart, and it rises up—a full arena! It just appears! They only use it for academy tournaments, demonstrations, and that sort of stuff. It holds, like, thousands of people."

Fletch gulped. His armpits were starting to sweat—and that just made him more anxious. "Wait, are you saying . . . ?"

"That's right!" Izzy chirped. "The Combatition takes place in front of students, professors, Squirebots—even townsfolk can get tickets! You'll be fighting in front of *everyone*."

Fletch nodded.

And after he nodded, he just about puked.

The day at Knights' Academy was busy—jammed full of class and combat. Fletch and Izzy's second class was a terribly boring geography course, taught by Professor Scapeland. She was a perpetually sleepy-looking woman who seemed to find geography even less interesting than the students did—which was saying a lot.

A History of Knights and Knighton wasn't much better. Professor Relik spent the first class lecturing about Ned Knightley and his many, many heroic deeds. Ned Knightley: the hero of the Battle of Golden Castle, a legend in the monster wars against Monstrox, the knight who made the ultimate sacrifice to protect Knighton. Fletch found it all fascinating, but it gave Zilgo a chance to again brag about his victory in the opening-day field-quest.

Combo Power Class was supposed to be a blast—all day long, Izzy had been telling Fletch how great it would be. But Fletch found it terrifying—he knew very little about NEXO Powers as it was, and Professor Ottofae only confused him further. Fletch gathered that the idea was that *three knights* could combine to download three separate NEXO Powers that would combine to form one single Combo NEXO Power.

But apparently, Combo NEXO Powers hadn't quite been perfected yet—and there was no telling what you were getting with these things. When Professor Ottofae mistakenly caused a three-ton hunk of butter to beam into the classroom, Fletch decided Combo Powers might not be for him . . .

Introduction to the Knight's Code: Basics of Knighthood saw the students, basically, reciting the Knight's Code over and over and over again. It put Fletch half to sleep, but he perked up on the way to the final class of the day: An Overview of Digital Magic.

Fletch had been looking forward to it all day. He hoped to learn about magic, and maybe even get some answers about *the feeling*.

Ava Prentis taught the class. She was only a second-year student, but she worked closely with the most famous knights in the land *and* Merlok 2.0.

"Welcome to class, students," Ava said. She spoke in a drawl that made her sound simultaneously really bored and insanely smart. Fletch immediately thought she was awesome.

Fletch sat down, excited. His foot steadily tapped the floor. No more combo powers, no more combat—it's *magic time*, he thought.

While reviewing the class attendance list, Ava paused at a name. "Izzy Richmond?"

Izzy's hand shot into the air. "Here! Present!"

Ava glanced up and frowned. "Tell your brother he owes me five pieces of Knighton gold."

"Will do!" Izzy replied cheerfully.

Ava dove into the inner workings of digital magic, and Fletch hung on her every word. She walked from monitor to monitor, pressing buttons, bringing up images of shields and powers. "It's digital magic that turns regular knights into NEXO KNIGHTS heroes. And someday, when you're out in battle—*I* may be the one sending you the Potent Pepper Power Axe that you so desperately need."

Fletch's hand shot up. Ava looked down at her list, then up at Fletch.

"Fletcher Bowman?" she asked.

"Yes."

"You have a question?"

"Yes."

"Okay."

"Will we learn about *real* magic in this class? Like, olden-days magic?"

Ava looked at Fletch curiously. "No. There is no reason. The only magician in the kingdom is Merlok."

"Oh," Fletch said. After a moment, he raised his hand again. "Can I ask another question?"

"Yes, Fletcher?"

"How do you know for sure there's only one magician in the kingdom?"

Ava shrugged. "It's a fact. There used to be a full Wizards' Council, but the members turned evil, one by one. Only Merlok was able to defeat them. And when he did, he was the only one left. So . . . like I said, just one."

"Oh," Fletch said. After another moment, he raised his hand again. "Um. One other question."

Ava sighed. "Yes, Fletcher?"

"Would you mind just calling me Fletch?"

Ava continued explaining all things digital magic, and Izzy caught Fletch's attention. Her eyes were wide as she mouthed the word "magician." After what happened in the catacombs yesterday, they were both thinking the same thing: Could there actually be *two* magicians in Knighton? And could Fletch be one of them?

"One thing to remember," Ava told the students, "is that *not* all of you will be great fighters. You may discover that your true calling is the study of technology."

"Perfect for Fletcher!" Zilgo hollered from the back of the room. "Zero danger!"

Fletch glanced back to scowl—but instead, his eyes just about popped out of his head. A jolt of terrified surprise shot through him, and he nearly shot out of his seat. Through the doorway, Fletch saw the Rogul hovering down the hallway.

"Izzy!" Fletch whispered. "It's out!"

"What?"

"The Rogul!" Fletch said, just barely keeping his voice below the level of a panicked scream. He quickly stood. His heart pounded as he felt the entire class watching him. *Oh no, oh no, oh no—what do I say?*

Izzy kept her head down, whispering, "Bathroom, bathroom, bathroom."

Ava noticed Fletch, standing up, looking totally freaked. "Yes, Fletcher?" she said tiredly.

"Ah, I have to go to the bathroom!" Fletch announced. The words tumbled out of his mouth.

Ava shrugged. "Well, I wouldn't want to stop you."

"Thanks!" Fletch said, and he was already halfway through the classroom. A moment later, he burst out into the hallway. Behind him, he heard chortling and snickering from the classroom.

Fletch spotted the Rogul zipping down the hall, emitting blue light and an electrical hum. He couldn't believe no one had come out to investigate yet.

"Rogul!" Fletch said.

The Rogul slowly turned, then quickly came rushing toward Fletch. Fletch saw that the Rogul was covered in his clothes—socks dangled from the statue's shoulders, and a pair of his underwear hung from its hooded head.

Fletch squeaked and quickly jammed the underwear into his pocket. "We need to get you back before anyone sees you!" Fletch said. "You're going to get me expelled!"

"GRUNT."

Fletch glanced in either direction. He needed to get all the way back to his dorm room—halfway across the academy. "Just follow me," Fletch said.

An instant later, Fletch was sprinting down the hall, and the Rogul was zooming behind him. At every classroom door, Fletch slid to a stop, peeked into the class, made sure it was clear, and then rushed ahead. The Rogul zipped behind, slamming into Fletch at every sudden stop.

Approaching his dormitory hall, Fletch turned the corner, and his heart leapt up into his throat. Principal

Brickland was marching down the hall! Fletch promptly doubled back—and promptly slammed into the Rogul.

"*GRUNT.*"

"Forget getting me expelled, you're going to get me killed!" Fletch said, rubbing his nose. "The Book of Monsters has been defeated, but Monstrox is still around! Principal Brickland will think I'm some sort of traitor who's helping bring monsters into the academy or something!"

Fletch flung open a nearby bathroom door. "Inside!"

"*GRUNT.*"

"You can't keep following me around! Look," Fletch said as he stepped into the bathroom. "This is *IN.*"

The Rogul hovered through the doorway, and Fletch quickly jumped back out, yanking the door shut behind him. Fletch was breathing hard as he stepped around the corner and—

BOOM!

Fletch collided with Principal Brickland. Fletch bounced off his armored chest. Brickland's eyes shot downward, surveying Fletch. "What's your name, novice student?" the principal snapped.

"Um. Fletcher. Fletcher Bowman," Fletch said, getting to his feet.

"And why might you be racing down my halls, Fletcher Bowman?"

"I'm just, um, just running a quick errand for— for Ava. I mean, Professor Ava. I mean, Professor Prentis."

"Ahh, an Overview of Digital Magic," Principal Brickland said. "All right, carry on. But slow your pace, student—understand?"

"Yes, sir," Fletch said. He was just stepping away, planning to wait for Brickland to leave before retrieving the Rogul, when Brickland said, "HALT!"

Fletch gulped. "Halt?"

"Yes, HALT! Do you smell that?"

"Um, no?" Fletch said. He was being honest. He didn't smell anything. Did the Rogul smell? Maybe a bit like the catacombs, Fletch thought, but not *really*. Principal Brickland would have to have, like, a superpowered nose to pick up that odor.

Principal Brickland sniffed suspiciously at the air. "It smells like—hmm—like Merlok. Like the *old* Merlok, when he was flesh and blood. It smells like . . . *magic*."

Fletch gulped. "Um, well, would that be so bad?" he asked after a moment.

"So bad?" the principal roared. "Magic in my academy? Would that be so bad!? I know you're only a first-year, so you don't know diddly yet—but *YES*, that *would* be SO BAD. Magic turns everyone evil! Everyone!"

"But what about Merlok?" Fletch asked.

Stomping forward, his face alight with something like stubborn fury, Principal Brickland said, "Merlok is the one exception. The *only* exception. Magic is evil, awful. Anyone that performs magic will be locked up, thrown behind bars! You understand?"

"Yes, sir," Fletch said. "Yes, sir. Completely."

"Good," Principal Brickland said. "There you go. A lesson learned, on your second day."

With that, the principal quickly marched away. Fletch waited a moment and then opened the door—just as the Rogul came drifting out. A long line of toilet paper was stuck to his swirling body.

Fletch groaned and shook his head. "Come on, Rogul . . ."

* * *

That night, Fletch and Izzy ate dinner in the cafeteria. The cafeteria was enormous and grand, but for the moment, Fletch had lost the ability to be impressed by the academy. He was sick with worry about the next day's battle competition. And he only became queasier and more anxious when he thought about Brickland saying magic turned people evil.

Fletch could always eat. He never turned down a meal, a snack, a bite, a spread, or a buffet. And he would eat *anything*. But now he just poked at his food, swirling around mashed potatoes and pushing peas back and forth across his plate. Izzy leaned in, about to ask what was wrong, when Zilgo sauntered past.

"Hey, Fletcher," Zilgo said. "I spoke with Captain Clash. I apologized about the whole fight today."

Fletch stabbed at a piece of ham.

"The professor said it was quite, *quite* kind of me," Zilgo said, leaning in and showing off his snide little smile. "*So kind* of me, in fact, that he thought you and I should have another go at it. So it'll be you and me at the Combatition tomorrow."

Fletch gritted his teeth and poked at the ham again. It was quickly turning to ham puree. *Great. Things just kept getting better . . .*

"Good luck, Fletcher," Zilgo said. He chuckled loudly as he strode away.

Fletch looked at Izzy. He was on the verge of a total freak-out. Izzy smiled. "Relax, buddy. Nothing is ever as bad you think it'll be!"

CHAPTER SEVEN

Nope.

It was *much, much* worse than Fletch had thought it would be. Fletch was in the process of being clobbered. And the clobbering was happening in front of a *thousand* people.

It was a shame, too, Fletch thought—because it was a beautiful morning. The sun was warm and bright, causing the entire Academy Arena to glow. And the Academy Arena *was* as awesome as Izzy had described. Early that morning, they had stood on one of the school's terraces and watched the ground open up and the Academy Arena appear. The grass split along perfectly trimmed lines, and the massive, glowing arena rose up like some great, hidden secret. It was so amazing that Fletch couldn't believe it was *real.*

Students, professors, and Squirebots now filled the Academy Arena grandstands, along with a smattering of city folks. Fletch couldn't believe there was so much interest in watching the first-year students fight. Apparently, ever since Jestro and the Book of Monsters began harassing the land, the citizens had taken a *huge* interest in their protectors, the NEXO KNIGHTS heroes. And an opportunity to get a glimpse of their *future protectors* was not to be missed!

Fletch heard a Squirebot's voice, calling out, peddling peanuts. Fletch wished he could be the one in the stands, chomping on snacks, relaxing—instead of in the middle of the arena, across from Ethan Zilgo.

Because Ethan Zilgo was beating the snot out of him.

And maybe worst of all, students were stuck with the weapon they had chosen the day before. That meant Fletch had a bow and arrow—a bow and arrow that he still didn't even know how to *use.* And there would be no help from NEXO Powers—they were strictly forbidden during Combatition. All combat was done the old-fashioned way: banging, clanging, bashing, and smashing.

Fletch wondered if Zilgo would mind standing still

for a few moments? Just for a minute or two, so that Fletch could figure out how this weapon operated and maybe, possibly, even fire one of these glowing blue arrows in the villain's general direction?

Not likely.

"You're not even making this fun!" Zilgo hollered, swinging his big blade. Fletch managed to lift his shield and block the blow—but he was sent sprawling back.

Fletch lifted an arrow and fumbled it. It fell to the stadium floor. He quickly glanced at Captain Clash, hoping he might stop the match, but Clash did not. Clash simply stared at Fletch, stern-faced. Fletch heard the crowd gasping and murmuring in pity.

Fletch didn't like that.

He didn't like being pitied.

He looked for Izzy, but she was gone . . .

She probably couldn't bear to watch me get knocked around, he thought. *Great. More pity.*

Fletch attempted to flee from Zilgo, but he could barely move in his armor. He lurched around the arena, feeling thick-legged and clumsy.

Zilgo shouted, "Stand still and let me hit you!"

Yeah, no thanks, Fletch thought. He would not simply stand still and allow himself to be knocked around.

Fletch gave up on the idea of defense for the moment: He threw his shield over his back, giving him two free hands. He raised the high-tech bow and managed to nock an arrow and draw back the bow. His fingers snapped open, and a glowing blue arrow spiraled through the air.

Fletch felt a rush of confidence—he had done it! He had fired an arrow!

But the rush did not last long. With a quick hack, Zilgo knocked the arrow from the air. Zilgo then rushed forward, swung, and sliced Fletch's bow in half.

Fletch was left holding a single arrow. He gawked at it, speechless. "Um . . ."

Zilgo raised the sword again—high and mighty and pretty darn scary.

Fletch was done flopping around like a fish. He dropped to one knee, yanked his shield from his back, and thrust it high into the air. If he was going to be clobbered, he could at last make it *appear* as if he had the first clue about how to defend himself.

Fletch held his arm out, stiff, and braced for the incoming blow. But what he didn't know, at that moment, was that Izzy had a plan of her own . . .

Minutes earlier, Izzy had rushed from the stadium. She couldn't stand watching Fletch get knocked around—she had to *do something*. She had raced back to the dormitory halls, snuck into Fletch's room, shouted hi to the Rogul (who was now back in the closet with *three* sheets tied around the door), and grabbed their newly found NEXO Power. The school was practically empty, so she had been able to race to Captain Clash's classroom. And there, she did something that she most definitely should *not* have done . . .

She took the power, and she inserted it into the Novix machine for scanning.

And at that very moment, far from the arena, inside the classroom—Izzy flipped a switch and beamed the power to Fletch.

Zilgo wore a vicious sneer. He held his sword high, enjoying the feeling of power—enjoying the gazing crowd.

But Zilgo enjoyed his moment a second too long.

With Fletch's shield raised to block the incoming attack, *it happened.* A beam shot up from the shield. It linked with the Novix system in midair. Pixels flew, and a symbol appeared. But it was not a golden symbol, as Fletch had seen in class. It was something different . . .

Fletch gasped as tremendous bursts of purple light erupted in the air above him. A swirling ball of silver energy slammed into his shield, entering it, filling it with power. Streaks of pink and purple light whirled around Fletch. Thick black smoke clouded the air.

Fletch felt a surge of energy the instant the strange power entered the shield. He saw Zilgo's mouth go slack in stunned disbelief.

Quickly, that disbelief turned to anger and rage. Using NEXO Powers in the Combatition was forbidden—and Fletch was officially a cheater.

Zilgo snarled, baring his teeth. He jabbed his sword, but Fletch dodged—whipping back his shield and swinging the arrow. Zilgo's mouth hung open—Fletch's arrow had sliced the sword clean in half!

Fletch whirled. Blue electricial power was flowing through his shield and his arrow. He swung the arrow again, and electricity sprung from the tip—zapping Zilgo and driving him backward.

The crowd *roared*.

Glancing around, Fletch saw Captain Clash. His eyes were narrowed, and there was something like fury etched in the deep, shadowy lines of his face.

Fletch realized what had happened. Izzy must have taken the power and sent it to him. And Fletch knew what he should do.

He should drop the shield to the ground and step away from it. He should march directly to the professor and tell him *everything*.

But Fletch heard the roar of the crowd and saw

Zilgo—nasty, cruel Zilgo—and for the first time in his *entire life*, Fletch felt powerful.

Captain Clash stood bolt upright. He scowled at Fletch then waved a hand. A squad of Squirebots rushed Fletch. Fletch swung the arrow, and streams of energy slammed into the bots, filling them with electricity, short-circuiting them, and hurling them back.

More Squirebots charged, and the result was the same. In just a few moments, Fletch had sent a dozen Squirebots flying. They were scattered across the arena, sizzling and sparking.

Ethan Zilgo slowly got to his feet. He had been humiliated—and Fletch knew then that Zilgo would be his enemy for a long, long time.

Fletch glanced back at the rows of first-year bleachers. He saw Izzy rushing up the steps, returning to her seat. She caught Fletch's eye and flashed a huge, conspiratorial grin.

And he was reminded that it was wrong.

It was irresponsible.

It was cheating.

It was dangerous.

But it was also *awesome*.

Fletch looked around the arena in astonishment. The

crowd was chanting his name: "Fletch! Fletch! Fletch! Fletch! Fletch!"

He had never felt so good. His heart surged. For once, he felt like he *belonged*. And then, a moment later, it all fell apart . . .

Electrical energy erupted from the arrow's tip. Fletch's arm swung wildly from side to side. The arrow was like a wand—a wand for directing destructive energy.

The arrow jolted and jerked, emitting long, streaming beams of light. The crowd's cheers turned to frightened cries as they saw Fletch had no control over the power. It was like gripping a gushing fire hose—all he could do was hold on.

With fright, he realized the electricity was moving toward the bleachers. Students cried out and rushed for the exits. A bolt of electricity shot through the stands, carving up a row of empty seats.

"Help!" Fletch cried. "I can't stop it!"

Fletch wrapped both hands around the arrow and managed to jerk it downward. Huge electrical charges blasted the stadium floor. Jagged cracks scorched the ground, splitting it open.

And then the power began to go out.

Everywhere.

The pixel-spotlights dimmed first, and then the loud-speaker squeaked and faded out. Finally, every last bit of electricity in the academy went out.

Izzy vaulted from the stands, hitting the stadium floor and rushing toward Fletch. He was wrestling with the arrow. "I'm coming!" she cried out.

The electricity erupted from the arrow like lightning. Izzy leapt and dodged the explosive energy. She slammed into Fletch, throwing her arms around him and tackling him.

The arrow slipped from Fletch's hand and dropped to the ground.

Fletch squirmed while Izzy held him down. Finally, the power began to wear off, and the shield dimmed.

Fletch looked around. Coils of smoke drifted up from the stands. The stadium floor was sliced open. A few frightened onlookers stumbled around, watching Fletch and Izzy with a mixture of confusion and fright.

"Izzy," Fletch whispered. "What did you do? What did I do?"

Izzy slowly shook her head as she climbed off her friend. "I just couldn't watch you get clobbered anymore . . ."

Suddenly, a voice erupted. "Armor off! Shields down!" Captain Clash was racing across the field, vaulting over the smoldering earth.

Principal Brickland followed close behind. His face was twisted with fury and rage. "My office. *Now!*"

Fletch had never felt worse in his life. Just thirty minutes earlier, students and citizens had been chanting his name, cheering him on—and now he sat across from Principal Brickland, certain that he was about to be kicked out of school. Izzy sat in the chair next to him. Her eyes were focused on the floor. The two friends couldn't even look at each other—there was nothing to say.

It was dusk, and Brickland's windowless office was nearly pitch-black. He lit a candle, then sat in his chair. He promptly stood back up, then sat down again, and then stood a final time. He was so enraged he didn't seem to know what to do with himself. But Fletch noticed something else. He didn't only seem angry—although, yes, he was most definitely furious. He also appeared *nervous*.

"Fletcher, Isabella, I assume you look quite frightened right now?" Brickland asked the two students. Before they could answer, Brickland roared, "I wouldn't know, because *I CAN'T SEE YOUR FACES!* Do you know why?"

"You lost your glasses?" Izzy asked.

"SHOVE A SHIELD IN IT, RICHMOND! I CAN'T SEE YOUR FACES BECAUSE YOU'VE SHUT DOWN ALL POWER IN THE ACADEMY AND IT'S NEARLY PITCH-BLACK!"

Principal Brickland again collapsed in his chair. Fletcher was sure now. There was fear in the principal's eyes. "Do you realize what've you done? In all my years . . . Never . . . Nothing so appalling . . . So unforgivable."

Fletch began to speak, but it took a moment to pull the words from his throat. It was like he was choking on a mix of shame and fear. "We found a NEXO Power, sir. We thought you'd be happy. Neither of us had any idea—"

"NEXO Power?" Brickland said. "You mean . . ." And then he trailed off, his words turning to an unsteady laugh that alarmed Fletch.

A moment later, there was a clattering in the hallway, and Ava came in from the darkness. Three Squirebots obediently followed. They carried a round, metallic pedestal that glowed orange.

Ava skipped any greetings. "Thankfully, this pedestal display retains its own backup power charge," she said. "Otherwise, he'd be lost."

"He?" Fletch asked, then remembered he most certainly should *not* be talking.

Ava gazed at Fletch sympathetically. "He," she said, "is Merlok 2.0."

Fletch sucked in a quick gasp of air. He was going to meet Merlok!

Ava turned a dial on the pedestal, and the orange, pixelated version of Merlok appeared. Fletch was staring at the greatest—*and only*—wizard in the kingdom. He would have been in awe if he weren't so ashamed.

From the pedestal, the glowing holographic Merlok fixed his eyes on Fletch and Izzy. "So these are the two. Very impressive. You managed to find—"

"A NEXO Power!" Izzy exclaimed. "I don't know why it caused so much—"

Merlok quickly cut her off. He shook his head. "Oh no, my dear. Not a NEXO Power. The opposite. What you found is a *Forbidden Power*. Something I've not seen in many, many years. This one is called Vicious Voltage."

Fletch glanced nervously at Izzy. *Forbidden Power?* He had no idea what a Forbidden Power was, but it certainly didn't sound good. Especially not that name: Vicious Voltage!

Merlok continued, and Fletch leaned forward. Merlok was talking about magic, and for a moment, despite his fear of expulsion, Fletch was fascinated. "Long ago, the Forbidden Powers were used by Monstrox in an attempt to destroy the realm. He was defeated by me, of course—and with a little help from the Wizards' Council, I suppose—"

"And some very brave knights," Brickland interrupted.

"The Forbidden Powers were destructive spells," Merlok continued. "They were outlawed by the Wizards' Council, then sealed in stone tablets by none other than *me*. I must admit, my memory is a bit scattered on this subject—still in pieces, you understand. But I knew the damage they could do—so I hid them across the kingdom and placed statues to guard them."

Fletch swallowed. *Statues. The Rogul!*

Brickland stood up, leaning forward like a coiled beast, ready to pounce. His hands gripped his desk so tight Fletch half expected it to crack. "I *fought* the villains that wielded the Forbidden Powers," Brickland growled. "They turned the members of the Wizards' Council evil, one by one. And now you've found a Forbidden Power and unleashed it within *my* academy! *On your third day of school!*"

Brickland furiously pounded the desk. The candle flickered out, and the only remaining light came from Merlok's glowing hologram. The wizard's voice changed pitch. He was the greatest and only wizard in the land, and he sounded *scared*. "The power," he said. "Oh, the power . . ."

Glaring at Fletch, Brickland got to the horrible heart of the matter. "You *must* understand what you've done. It's not just a few school days without lights, without screens. No, no. With the exception of the king's castle, this academy is the most well-protected, well-armed building in the kingdom. And you have *shut down our defenses entirely.* I've had to send every fourth-year squire to guard the walls and patrol the city!"

Fletch's stomach flipped. He suddenly understood the awful repercussions of what they'd done. He understood why Brickland and Merlok were so scared.

"This academy contains every young knight in the land," Merlok said. "Young knights who are being trained to protect the kingdom. If Monstrox had any idea that the academy was defenseless, he could destroy us all. And that would, of course, be quite bad."

Izzy's chin dipped to her chest. She tucked her elbows in tight against her, gripped by guilt.

Fletch, too, wanted to look away. His stomach felt sick and there was a thickness in his throat. But he knew how wrong they had been—and the least he could do was look Brickland in the eye as he reprimanded them.

"Are we . . . expelled?" Fletch finally asked.

The principal turned away. "I will discuss that with King Halbert shortly. If it was up to me, you'd be gone already."

Fletch gulped. *The king! The king was going to know what he had done!*

Fletch slowly stood. "Sir, I was the one who led us to find the power. You told us that knights should stick together. Izzy was only doing what I asked. Please, only expel me."

"Oh, how *noble* of you, young Bowman," Principal Brickland said sarcastically. "Each of you, to your rooms—directly. I would have you escorted, but half the academy is busy trying to repair the damage you've done."

Fletch and Izzy quietly stood. Ava offered a kindly smile, but Fletch was too embarrassed to return it.

As they left, Fletch glanced back at Merlok. The digital wizard watched him for a moment, staring into his eyes and—Fletch felt—almost staring into his soul. And then Merlok flickered away . . .

Shame.

Despair.

That was all Fletch felt walking back to his dorm.

His feet dragged as he trudged down the hall. The dread in his stomach was so heavy, it felt like it was weighing him down.

Suddenly, Izzy clutched Fletch's arm. Fletch snapped to and turned to his friend. Her face was snowy white, like she had just seen a ghost. "Fletch, with the academy's defenses down . . ."

"I know," Fletch muttered. "Monstrox could attack. I feel sick enough. You don't need to remind me . . ."

"No. *Worse.* Someone in the catacombs *wanted* that power. And *we* took it from them. Whoever was trying to get that power could come here now. If they could sense it, like you could, that would lead them directly to—"

"Mr. Captain Clash's classroom!" Fletch exclaimed. "To the Novix!"

Fletch realized that he and Izzy were both thinking the exact same thought: They should go back to their dorms, as ordered. They weren't knights. They were just kids, *way* in over their heads.

But there was something much bigger happening. Something *no one* understood. And they had to stop it . . .

They didn't say another word. They just raced toward Captain Clash's classroom.

CHAPTER EIGHT

letch's heart pounded as they darted down the darkened halls. They came to Captain Clash's classroom and burst inside. Fletch expected to see some sort of catastrophe—but he didn't.

Relief flooded through him as they entered. The room looked the same as it had the day prior, when Zilgo armor-bashed Fletch during the first day of class.

In the Novix machine, Fletch saw the Forbidden Power: Vicious Voltage. He still had trouble believing that's what it was: *forbidden*. The word hammered home just how *wrong* what they had done was.

The room glowed blue from the power in the machine.

It was the only electrical source in the entire academy now. The only other light came from the moon, visible through the huge reinforced window that ran along one side of the room.

Fletch thought it odd that a room built for combat would feel so *exposed*, but he had read that just one year earlier, after Jestro and the Book of Monsters first attacked, Principal Brickland redesigned the room. Brickland thought it important that the students could see the city on the horizon: a reminder of what they were training to protect.

"The power is still here," Izzy said as she carefully approached the humming shield. "Ava and Merlok are probably trying to figure out what to do with it."

Fletch glanced around nervously. There were no knights here. Not even any third- or fourth-year students to guard the power. They've all been sent out: some to the city, some to guard the academy walls.

"We have to tell Brickland and Merlok," Fletch said. "I'm certain those skeletal knights are coming for the power. Though I'm not sure they could get in here on their own. They didn't seem all that bright . . ."

"I bet they're not on their own," Izzy said. "I bet they serve an ancient knight in black-and-rust armor who rides a rotting, skeletal Pegasus."

Fletch, for the first time in what felt like forever, chuckled. "That's a pretty specific guess, Izzy."

"It's no guess. Look . . ."

Fletch turned to the window. He felt a freezing, frigid fear—starting at the tip of his spine and cracking like splintering ice down to his feet.

It was just a flash of something, at first, flying over the city. But it grew larger as it approached. The Pegasus' bony wings flapped, and a knight, in armor of black and rust, rode atop.

This soaring nightmare glided through the night sky, then swung toward the academy. It flew over the academy walls—and of course, no alarms were sounded because there was no electricity to power the alarms.

It was coming for them.

For the Forbidden Power.

The steed's massive, bony wings beat the air, and it picked up speed—whooshing toward the huge window. The knight of black and rust drew a lance. High above, clouds shifted, and suddenly he was soaked in yellow moonbeams.

The lance was jagged, splintered—and appeared to be made of bone.

KRAK!

The lance punctured the glass, and it was like the whole room exploded. Izzy did not move. She only watched. At the last instant, Fletch grabbed her—yanking her to the floor as the undead steed and the knight of black and rust came crashing into the room.

It felt like a sudden, strange earthquake ripping through the academy. The horse's wings beat twice, causing debris to scatter and whip about. Wind tore through the window, rolling off the training grounds.

"I am Baron von Bludgeonous," the knight said as he dismounted from his scary steed. He looked over the two students. "And I've come for the power."

Fletch was paralyzed as he watched this living nightmare march toward the Novix machine. With one tremendous blow, Baron von Bludgeonous' bony hand punched through it. He dug around inside, yanking out wires, and finally lifted out the Forbidden Power.

He then turned around and swung his lance through the training suits. His bony weapon cut through the armor, rendering them completely useless.

Fletch trembled as he stood. He tried to keep his body stiff, firm, brave—but he knew he was quaking. He concentrated on his words—he didn't want his voice to quiver. "You can't take that," he said firmly.

The baron jerked around, and his eyes seemed to dart about and then locked on Fletch.

Without meaning to, Fletch took a step back. Izzy got to her feet, standing tall beside her friend.

Baron von Bludgeonous stomped across the room, and in an instant, he loomed over the two students. Baron von Bludgeonous reached up to his steel helmet. With a metal clink, he raised it. He revealed not a human face but something so freaky that Fletch's breath caught in his throat.

Small spheres of swirling darkness hovered inside the knight's two eye sockets. The knight was only thick bone, no skin—a skeleton but monstrously oversized and heavily armored.

"I smell it," the undead knight hissed. "I can smell it in your blood, young one. *Magic.*"

"Fletch doesn't smell! You smell!" Izzy shouted, and she punched the villain's iron chest plate. Instantly, she leapt back, hopping from foot to foot, gripping her hand and muttering in pain.

The knight's bony mouth formed a smile. "Brave girl. But you, boy—I smell something else on you, too. *Cowardice.* I have no need to fear you. You're just children. But I wonder—should I do away with you both, to be safe . . . ?"

"DON'T MOVE!"

Izzy and Fletch whirled around. The knight glanced at the door, and his swirling black eyes turned red.

It was Brickland, holding a long iron sword. "Drop the Vicious Voltage, and leave. Now."

Baron von Bludgeonous chuckled—a sound like a blade scraping away winter ice. He about-faced and returned to his steed.

Brickland ran toward the undead knight. He swung, but Baron von Bludgeonous thrust the power forward, blocking the blow. A burst of white-hot energy sparked, lighting up the room. Brickland continued swinging, unleashing a flurry of attacks. But the villain blocked each blow, and the entire room seemed to hum electric.

"Your attempts are futile," the baron said. "But I respect your swordsmanship, so I will not destroy you. But soon your time will come. This academy will be annihilated. This kingdom will fall."

With that, the undead knight slammed his armored boot into Brickland's chest, and Brickland staggered to the floor. Baron von Bludgeonous mounted his undead steed, jerked the reins, and the Pegasus leapt through the window. Fletch watched the glow of the Forbidden Power fading into the distance as the enemy soared through the sky.

A voice said, "Oh boy. Captain Clash will *not* like what happened to his classroom."

It was Ava. She looked the room over and then glanced at Fletch and Izzy. Fletch looked away—he couldn't bear it.

Brickland sucked air as he stood. "Ava, have Merlok call the other knights back to the academy. As quickly as the Fortrex can move."

Ava nodded and hurried off.

"What can we do?" Izzy asked.

Brickland's face—with its look of fury and disappointment—made Fletch's hair stand on end. "You can pack your bags," Brickland said.

"You can't go!" Izzy exclaimed.

Fletch spun around. "Did you see what happened back there? Did you see that horrible *monster*? The whole kingdom is in danger, and it's my fault!"

Izzy slumped down in Fletch's desk chair. She anxiously tapped at the frames of her glasses while the Rogul hovered silently in the corner of Fletch's dorm. The statue's swirling blue energy provided just enough light for Fletch to pack his bag.

"But you have an important power, Fletch," Izzy pleaded. "A power I can't understand."

"And a power I obviously can't control," Fletcher said coldly.

"But people need to know about it!"

"You heard what Brickland said. Magic turns people evil. I'll turn evil, like the Wizards' Council did."

Izzy quickly stood. "And that's why you should stay," she said, taking her friend's hand. "Tell Merlok. He'll understand. He can help you."

Fletch saw the look in her eyes, wide and pleading. And he realized it was *her* that he would miss most. All that he had seen in the past few days: the astonishing academy, the wondrous digital weapons, the mysterious catacombs, the holographic wizard. He had seen a world he never knew existed—a world so much bigger and more astounding and wonderful than he imagined was possible. But it was the tiny, undersized, kick-butt Izzy—his friend—that made him want to stay.

But that wasn't enough to make him do the wrong thing. And he knew that just by being here, he was putting the academy—and the kingdom—in danger. The only way to keep them safe was to go back to the orphanage, and never follow *the feeling* again.

Fletch threw his bag over his shoulder. "I'm leaving, Izzy. I have to. Good-bye." He quickly turned to the door so she wouldn't see the look of heartbreak on his face.

CRUNCH!

Fletch spun around just in time to see the Rogul come bursting out of the corner. Wood exploded outward as the door shattered.

"GRUNT."

"Sorry, Rogul. I'm going."

The Rogul drifted toward the wall. He slammed right into it, the whole room trembled, and then he bounced off. Again, the Rogul bumped into the wall, and again he rebounded off.

Izzy gasped. Sudden realization appeared on her face. "The Rogul knows!" Izzy said. "He had the Forbidden Power! He must know how to get it back!"

"So go tell Brickland," Fletch said.

With a swift tug, Izzy yanked Fletch's bag from his shoulder, and it thumped to the floor. "Fletch, the Rogul is loyal to *you*. He follows *you*. He can lead us to the tablet and the power! You and me, buddy—we're the ones who can save the day. It's perfect! It's classic!"

It was such insanity that Fletch could only shake his head and smile. The two of them, the two who had *caused* all these problems, saving the day? Fletch laughed. They were the *last* people who should be trying to fix things.

"Fletch!" Izzy barked. "Listen! I can't stop you from leaving the academy. But you *need* to do this first. If you quit before you put everything back right again, well—"

"Well what?" Fletch asked angrily.

"Well then, I happen to think you're *exactly* what that awful knight monster thing said you were. A coward."

Fletch felt like he had been slugged in the stomach. His mouth opened, but he didn't know how to respond. He had always wondered if he *was* a coward. In a small way, in the back corner of his mind, he had always felt like one. And now his friend—his only friend—had just said it. Out loud! There was the possibility she was only trying to motivate him.

Fletch scowled. "Fine. Let's go. Quickly."

"But one thing," Izzy said. "I *won't* travel with you on a grand kingdom-saving mission if you're going to be a moody grump the whole time."

Fletch crossed his arms and stood stiff. "Well, I can't help it. That's just—"

Izzy poked Fletch in his side, cutting him off. Fletch tried to resist, but he laughed.

"Okay, okay!" Fletch said, throwing up his arms. "Come on, buddy, let's go save the day. You too, Rogul."

Izzy grinned. "That's better."

With that, Izzy and the Rogul followed Fletch out the door, off to stop Baron von Bludgeonous, retrieve the Forbidden Power, and save the kingdom.

The hallway was quiet and still. It was past curfew now—and even if it wasn't, Principal Brickland surely had informed all students not to leave their rooms until power was returned and security was restored.

"We need weapons!" Izzy whispered as they crept down the hall. "We can't take on that huge, foul Baron von Bludgeonous without weapons."

"Which weapons?" Fletch asked. "Bludgeonous destroyed the training suits, and I don't have a clue where to get a real suit of armor. How about you, Rogul—any ideas?"

"*GRUNT.*"

"Right . . ."

Suddenly, Izzy perked up—Fletch knew she had something up her sleeve. She said, "We need a weapon that belonged to the greatest knight of the ancient era. We need a weapon that belonged to a knight who represented all that is good. We need . . . Ned Knightley's Silver Sword of Silverness!"

"You think that matters?" Fletch asked. "That the weapon is old and ancient and belonged to a great guy?"

Izzy shrugged. "Probably not, but I don't know what other weapon to go after. Come on, *to the hall!*"

Unfortunately, as Fletch and Izzy soon discovered, the Hall of Knights wasn't empty. Turning the corner, they saw someone standing at the pedestal where Ned Knightley's Silver Sword of Silverness was now displayed.

Fletch groaned. It was the *last* person he wanted to see. He would rather have bumped into Principal Brickland!

Izzy scowled. "Zilgo! He's admiring his prize. He found it, like, two whole days ago. Geez . . ."

Fletch knew they needed that sword. Izzy was right—there was no way they could face Baron von Bludgeonous empty-handed. "Let's try talking to him," Fletch said. "Maybe he'll understand."

Fletch ordered the Rogul to stay put. Then he and Izzy marched down the hall. The sculptures of brave ancient knights loomed over them. Fletch felt like the sculptures were watching him—judging him—asking if he had what it took to be a knight.

Zilgo whirled as he heard their footsteps. "You two!" he said. "Don't you ever learn?"

"What are you doing here?" Izzy asked.

"Admiring the sword."

"Well, your admiring time is up," Izzy said. "We're taking that sword. So step off."

Zilgo shot them a smug glare. "What? Taking it with you as some sort of memento? A parting gift? You're done at this academy. Everyone knows." Zilgo opened his hands and stepped forward. "Izzy, Izzy, Izzy . . . You never should have joined up with this *orphan*. You and I, Richmond, we would have made a good team."

Izzy began to speak, but Fletch stepped forward— his blood was practically boiling. "Zilgo, we have no time for your nonsense! Get out of the way."

"One more step, *Fletcher*, and I'll tell Brickland you attacked me."

Fletch stepped back. He had never won by fighting. He wasn't a fighter. If anything, he was a thinker. He raised his arm and clenched his hand.

"What's that, a commoner dance move?" Zilgo said with a narrow smirk. But an instant later, the smirk was gone—replaced by a terrified stare. The Rogul was whisking down the hall. He zipped past Fletch and Izzy, and came to a swirling stop just in front of Zilgo.

The statue leaned in, looming over Zilgo, his stone face almost touching the boy's forehead. The boy began to stammer. "What-wha-wha—"

"Zilgo, this is my friend, the Rogul," Fletch said, taking a confident stride forward. "The Rogul would like it if we could borrow the sword. So could we? Pretty please? With a cherry on top?"

"And you should probably *not* tell anyone," Izzy chimed in. "Wouldn't want to wake up and see this big dude in your dorm room, would you?"

Zilgo took a few frightened steps back. He glanced from Fletch, to Izzy, to the Rogul, and back to Fletch again. And then he took off, sprinting down the corridor. He stumbled, nearly smashed into a sculpture, regained his footing, and threw a final terrified glance back at the Rogul. And the next moment, he was gone.

Izzy grinned at Fletch, then quickly removed the sword from its pedestal. Moments later, Fletch and Izzy had opened the secret passageway, and they were again descending into the catacombs . . .

CHAPTER NINE

Fletch and Izzy sprinted through the catacombs, doing their best to follow the Rogul, but the strange statue was *flying*. It was like they had let a windup toy go, and now they couldn't stop it.

"We'll never keep up at this pace!" Izzy cried.

"Rogul!" Fletch shouted. "Slow down!"

The Rogul halted. Suddenly, he was hovering back toward them.

"*GRUNT.*"

"What's he grunting about now?" Izzy wondered.

The Rogul hovered up, then down, up, then down— like he was trying to get them to notice something.

"Look," Izzy said, pointing. On the back of the Rogul's body, two of the stones had stopped swirling. They jutted out, floating in place.

Fletch got down on one knee and peered closer. "They're footholds. Like hover bike pegs!" he said excitedly.

Fletch stuck his foot onto the stone and hoisted himself up, gripping the Rogul's stone back. The statue emitted a soft grunt, and then Izzy climbed up as well—and they were off. Fletch's hair whipped about and Izzy's curls were a stream of blond as the Rogul zoomed down the catacomb tunnels at holo-rail speeds.

The Rogul's stone brain simply knew where to go: He took every turn, every corner, every split of the long catacombs at top speed, never slowing down. The Rogul breezed through cobwebs. Rats darted as the trio zoomed above them.

"He's like our own personal navigation system!" Izzy exclaimed, then quickly snapped her mouth shut. She had nearly swallowed a bug. Barf.

Fletch had a wide grin on his face. The speeding twists and turns mixed with the magical feeling in his stomach—and for a brief moment, he forgot all about the danger and just enjoyed the adventure.

"How far do you think we've gone?" Izzy shouted.

"Miles and miles!" Fletch shouted back.

And then, with zero warning, the Rogul came to a sudden stop. Fletch and Izzy slammed into the Rogul's back and bounced off, tumbling to the damp ground.

Rubbing his nose, Fletch sat up. "Rogul, buddy, we need to teach you how to slow down . . ."

Izzy spotted a ladder, similar to the one they used to enter the catacombs. Fletch began to climb, and Izzy followed. She checked to make sure she still had Ned Knightley's Silver Sword of Silverness by her side.

When Fletch reached the top, he half expected some magic seal to crack open above him. But there was no magic seal, no sewer grate, and no manhole cover at the top. Just solid brick.

Fletch pushed at it, and felt it move—but only slightly. Izzy braced herself against the side of the shaft, and together, they were able to lift the heavy brick.

Fletch quickly scrambled up and turned to help Izzy, but saw she had already hoisted herself over. Next came the Rogul, hovering up through the hole.

After sliding the brick back into place, they saw they were on the streets of Knightonia. The moon provided the only light. The streets were quiet. Fletch suspected that word of the threat to the city had caused everyone to stay indoors. Again, he felt like a fool—the whole city was shut down because of his actions.

"Now what?" Izzy asked.

As she spoke, the Rogul slowly drifted forward. Fletch and Izzy followed. Coming around the corner, Fletch's stomach just about flipped—he felt it immediately. They were close to the Forbidden Power . . .

The Rogul raised an arm and pointed to the crumbling old mansion. The surrounding buildings were run-down and appeared abandoned. The mansion was darker than everything nearby, giving it a menacing air. A tall brick wall encircled it. Atop the brick wall were strange red vines, unlike anything Fletch had ever seen.

"Thorneries," Izzy said, "Razor-sharp, to keep out intruders."

What kind of mansion needs to keep out intruders that badly? Fletch wondered. And he quickly realized: the type of mansion that they needed to sneak into. The type of mansion that's home to a villain like Baron von Bludgeonous.

It looked impregnable. The walls were impossible to climb over. Fletch and Izzy snuck all the way around, looking for some way in, but they saw nothing. There was a single gate in front—but a dozen skeletal guards, their bony frames hidden beneath long cloaks, guarded it.

Returning to the rear wall, Fletch felt the cool brick. "The only way in is over this wall . . . or through it."

"THROUGH."

Fletch whirled around. Had he heard right? Had the Rogul just spoken? Fletch was about to open his mouth to express his shock, when—

THUMP!

Bricks flew and rock crumbled as the Rogul slammed his hand into the wall. With one blow, the Rogul had punched a person-sized hole in the brick.

"Guess we found our entrance," Izzy said with a happy shrug.

"But we're supposed to be quiet!" Fletch said. "Baron von Bludgeonous and his guards can't know we're here!"

"Then we better move quickly," Izzy said, stepping through the crumbling brick opening.

Fletch followed, and the Rogul, of course, followed Fletch. Entering the large lawn that surrounded the mansion, Fletch was overcome by a sense of sadness. The entire place oozed a feeling of loss. The lifeless and yellowed grass crunched with every step. Trees dotted the yard, but they were rotten and pale with long gray limbs.

And ahead of them was the stone mansion itself. The entire thing looked like it was from another time, as if it had been transplanted there—yanked from some other world or kingdom. The mansion had two separate wings—the first was two stories high, and the second much taller. At the corner of the second wing was a huge, round spire. High at the top of the spire was a single window. Colors danced in the window. It was the only light that came from the mansion.

Izzy whistled as she eyed the scene. "Could use a gardener. And a painter. And just, like, *a lot* of sprucing up."

"Hey," Fletch whispered. "Do you hear that?"

"Yep," Izzy said. She unsheathed Ned Knightley's blade. "Incoming bad guys."

Fletch heard one knight growl and point. "I think the noise came from there!"

Three knights rushed across the lawn—and then there was the glistening of silver in the darkness. Izzy swung. The leading knight practically disappeared—in an instant, he had crumbled to a pile of bones.

Izzy swung twice more, and two more skeletal knights fell.

"That was close," Fletch said. He spun toward the Rogul. "*You have to stay here.* Okay? *Stay. Here.* Do you understand?"

The Rogul made no movement to indicate whether he understood. Groaning, Fletch reached up and grabbed the Rogul's hand and led him behind a large dead tree. "Here. Okay? Stay. Here. Behind this tree."

Fletch took a step away, and the Rogul followed.

"NO!" Fletch barked. *"You can't come!* You already alerted the guards once!"

The Rogul's head lowered. Fletch took a second step, and this time, the Rogul did not follow.

"I think you made the Rogul sad," Izzy said as she and Fletch crept through the tall, dead grass. Fletch didn't have time to worry about the Rogul's feelings—he was too busy worrying whether or not Baron von Bludgeonous knew they were coming . . .

"How do we find the power?" Izzy whispered.

"I can still sense it. The way I did before. But I don't know how we get inside."

There were holes and cracks in the mansion's crumbling walls, but they were too narrow to enter. Darkness seemed to leak from them. Rounding the corner, they spotted Baron von Bludgeonous' undead Pegasus. It was tied up in a crooked, creaking stable.

"Uh, let's go the other way," Izzy said, turning away from the chilling winged horse.

"We can try the roof!" Fletch said suddenly. "Maybe we can find a window or something then."

Twisted, dead vines and moss crawled up the side of the mansion. Fletch scaled the wall easily: He had often climbed the rocky seaside cliffs in Salt City, and this wasn't much different.

Izzy, however, hadn't done much climbing in her fancy Auremville manor. As she clambered up onto the roof, Ned Knightley's Silver Sword of Silverness slipped from her belt and dropped to the grass below.

"The sword!" she exclaimed.

Fletch peered over the edge of the roof. More skeletal knights were rounding the corner.

"We'll have to go on without it," Fletch said.

Creeping forward, they saw that the roof was dotted with holes and gashes. Small pools of stale water had formed from the last rain. In other spots, water dripped through. Fletch was reminded that Baron von Bludgeonous was not any sort of *living* creature who worried about things like warmth or rain or mansion-ruining mold.

Noise drifted from someplace near the center of the mansion. They slowly crawled toward it. The roof creaked beneath them. Soon they were overlooking the second floor of the house. Peering through, they saw it: the Forbidden Power.

It was at the center of a long room. It was once a large living room or such, Fletch figured, but it now looked like a throne room. A long bloodred carpet stretched along the floor below them. They could not see the entire room—but at the center, beneath them, was the Power.

Two dozen skeletal knights filled the room. Every few moments, one would creep forward and curiously inspect the tablet. And then—*ZAP*—the skeletal knight would be shocked and stumble back.

"Not too bright, are they?" Izzy whispered.

Fletch shook his head. "They're not. But Baron von Bludgeonous seems to be, and I don't see him . . ."

Izzy leaned forward, trying to get a better view.

"Careful!" Fletch whispered.

"I got it, I got it," Izzy said, and then . . .

CREAK!

A frown flashed across Izzy's face. "Fletch," she said. "I'm really sorry."

"Sorry about what?" Fletch began to say, but he didn't finish because the roof—*CRACK!*—collapsed. The ancient wood snapped and broke, and Fletch and Izzy tumbled through.

They landed in a heap. Sitting up, rubbing their wounds, they saw skeletal knights surrounded them.

A voice growled. "We have guests . . ."

Fletch and Izzy turned to see Baron von Bludgeonous sitting on his throne.

"Is that a bone throne?" Izzy whispered. "Tell me he has a bone throne."

Baron von Bludgeonous chortled. "Oh yes. *Now.* Say what you like. Say it all—because after tonight, you will never say anything again . . ." He rose from his bone throne. "Welcome to my castle . . ."

Fletch and Izzy got to their feet. Bits of crumbled roof were scattered at their feet. Glowering, Fletch said, "This isn't a castle. This is just a lame, crumbling old house."

Baron von Bludgeonous stepped toward Fletch. His steps were heavy and hard. He leered, revealing chipped and ancient fangs.

"Why . . . ?" Fletch managed to say. "Why did you take the power?"

"Let *me* ask *you* a question," Baron von Bludgeonous said. "Why do you attend the Knights' Academy?"

"To train as knights," Izzy said proudly.

"So you can fight the great enemy known as Monstrox," Baron von Bludgeonous said. "Is that also correct?"

Izzy barked, "So what?"

Baron von Bludgeonous made a revolting giggling sound—like his throat couldn't produce proper laughter. "You are so lucky," he said. "You have an eager enemy. I had to *find* a foe. You see, I was a knight, like you hope to be. But I was a knight many years ago, during the peaceful times, before the silly NEXO Powers."

"The golden era," Izzy said.

Baron von Bludgeonous laughed. This time, it sounded like something choking. "Golden era? Golden?! Is that what they call it at your school? It was the *worst* possible time to be a knight."

Baron von Bludgeonous extended his hand, opened it to reveal nothing—and then snapped it shut. "There were no enemies! And no enemies meant no battling, no questing, and *no glory*. All the things that makes a knight a *knight*."

Fletch couldn't understand. "You'd rather fight than have people living happily in peace?"

A cruel and twisted grin appeared on Baron von Bludgeonous' face. "Now you're catching on. I left Knightonia, seeking combat and glory. But instead, I found Monstrox. I happily joined his army. I fought the Halbert family, and I battled the Wizards' Council and the great knights. But soon I found something more powerful than even Monstrox . . ."

Fletch's heart pounded in his chest. "You mean . . . ?"

"*Forbidden Powers* . . ." Baron von Bludgeonous said. "And with them came everlasting *death*. It keeps me going, dead-but-not-dead—*forever*."

Fletch shivered. Baron von Bludgeonous radiated

with the chill of the unknown. But Fletch sensed something there, inside the villain. Wanting. Desire. *Thirst.*

Suddenly, he understood . . .

"But to stay alive—or to stay *undead*—you need more Forbidden Powers, don't you?" Fletch asked. "And that's why you searched for this one?"

Baron von Bludgeonous nodded. "You *are* bright. Yes. And now that I have it, I will use it to further my plan . . . Corruption! Decay! I will plunge all of Knighton into darkness, and then I will take what is rightfully mine . . ."

"Yours?" Izzy asked.

"Indeed," Baron von Bludgeonous growled. "I will take my rightful place as king! I will replace that old fool Halbert. I will rule over a kingdom of the undead."

A heavy silence hung in the room, only broken when the skeletal knights began to clap.

"Great plan, B!" one roared in approval.

"You're the boss!" another called out.

"Don't hurt us, please!" a third added.

Baron von Bludgeonous glared at the knights for a moment. Then his horrible gaze returned to Fletch and Izzy. "Pardon my minions. They aren't particularly sharp. It's the problem with skeleton soldiers—brains are lacking."

"We noticed," Izzy said.

"But you, boy, you're not lacking," Baron von Bludgeonous said as he crept toward Fletch. "Quite the opposite. You discovered the power when my entire army of knights searching the lands could not. Somehow you, a first-year student, simply found it."

Fletch was trembling. "It was just an accident."

Baron von Bludgeonous chuckled. "An accident? And is that also how you found my castle—"

"Mansion," Izzy interrupted. "House. Lodge. Shack. *Not* a castle."

Baron von Bludgeonous ignored her. "*Fletch*, boy, I believe you may yet prove useful. There are other Forbidden Powers, and you may be able to help me find them."

Good, fine, whatever, Fletch thought. *Anything to buy some time and figure a way out of this.*

Baron von Bludgeonous abruptly turned and marched back to his throne. "Knights!" he barked. "Take them to the dungeon. Lock them up and guard them well. I will take no chances! Or, well, very *few* chances!"

CHAPTER TEN

It was true: Baron von Bludgeonous had turned this old house into something like his own personal castle. And Fletch and Izzy were being led to his own personal dungeon . . .

The skeletal knights nudged them down the stairs, where the air became damp and musty. "The Rogul could help us," Fletch whispered as a guard poked his back. "We could *really* use a giant punching statue monster right now."

"You had to go and scold him! You made him all sad!" Izzy said.

They stepped off the stairs, into the basement

dungeon. The knights' swords poked at their backs, prodding them forward.

"I'm going, I'm going!" Izzy barked. "Ease up on the poking!"

It was once a simple basement, but it now looked and felt like a medieval dungeon, from the time before technology ruled Knighton. Empty prison cells lined one side of the dungeon.

"*Innnnsideeee,*" the knight in charge said, nudging them toward an open cell.

Fletch and Izzy reluctantly entered. A heavy clang echoed as the knight slammed the door shut. Fletch watched the knight in charge lock the door and then hang the key chain from his hipbone.

Hanging on one wall, behind the skeletal knights, were ancient weapons from *before* the time of NEXO Powers: iron maces, bronze axes, steel swords, and a bow and arrow. Cobwebs clung to them. Fletch stared at the weapons: so close, yet so far away.

High above Fletch and Izzy was a small, narrow window, looking out on the mansion's backyard. The window was covered in heavy bars. Fletch dug one foot into the brick wall and leapt up, grabbing the bars, lifting himself so he could peek outside.

He squinted, hoping to spot the Rogul—but his brick foothold cracked and he tumbled to the cell floor.

Fletch sat up, dusted himself off, and scooted next to Izzy. They each lifted up their legs, curling them tight—backs to the wall.

They exchanged downtrodden glances. They didn't have to speak the words—the looks on their faces said it all: defeat.

They were far from the academy. No one knew where they were. And, worst of all, the Forbidden Power was in Baron von Bludgeonous' possession.

"I really wish I didn't drop the sword," Izzy said with a heavy sigh. "Could use that sword right now. Or a mace, or an axe, or a morning star. Could really use *any* sort of weapon right now . . ."

"And I really wish I hadn't made the Rogul sad," Fletch added. "Could also use him right now . . ."

A chill drifted in through the bars, and Fletch wrapped his arms around himself. Izzy shoved her hands into her pockets. A moment later, she slipped one hand out: It held a photo.

A sad little smile appeared on Fletch's face. It was an autographed photo of Izzy's brother, Lance. It was what Lance had been offering to the students the morning he dropped Izzy off at the academy. It was only a few days ago, but to Fletch, it felt like a lifetime. Falling from the train. Meeting Izzy.

Izzy hung her head and let out a long, low sigh. "My brother is a pain in the butt and a diva," she said, her voice soft. "But at least he's a *real knight*. I'm just a pretender. A phony . . ."

Fletch raised an eyebrow. "Hey, Izzy, how long have the men and women in your family been famous knights?"

Izzy shrugged. "A long time. Way back."

Fletch grinned, snatched the photo from Izzy's hands, and leapt to his feet. "Ahem! Excuse me!" Fletch called out. "Guard! *Skeletal-knight guard in charge!*"

The head knight turned. *"Siiiiilence."*

"Sure, sure, silence. But one second. You see my friend here? She's a *Richmond.*"

Izzy sighed. "Fletch, why would they care? It's just a stupid name. It doesn't mean anything . . ."

"They're knights," Fletch whispered. "I mean, now they're all bony-bony. But they *used* to be knights."

The knight in charge looked at Fletch blankly. Its hollow eyes revealed nothing.

"Rich-mond," Fletch repeated.

Still nothing.

Undeterred, Fletch held up the picture. "See, this is *Lance Richmond*. He's the most famous knight in the land."

Suddenly, the knight in charge leaned close. In the darkness of the hollow eyes, Fletch saw a spark of something—awareness.

Another knight barked, "Lance! TV host! Famous!"

"And this photograph is *autographed*," Fletch said, tapping the picture. "Pretty cool, huh? Come here, take a look."

The knights began to rush toward the cell, but the knight in charge held up a bony hand, and they all halted. The knight in charge took another step forward. The key chain clattered against his bone.

Fletch held the photo through the bars, like he was trying to feed a skittish pet. "Go on, you can have it," Fletch said.

Izzy slowly approached the bars. She watched as the knight reached forward to take the picture.

She glanced at Fletch, eyebrows raised. Were they thinking the same thing? Fletch nodded. They were . . .

Izzy took another step forward. And then, just as the knight in charge grasped the photograph, Izzy grabbed him by the back of his skull.

"Gotcha!" Izzy said, and then—

SLAM!

She yanked the knight forward, bashing his head into the bars. At the same instant, Fletch's hand shot out and stole the keys.

"Got 'em!" Fletch said. He quickly jammed the keys into the lock and spun them. The knights rushed the cell.

"I got this," Izzy said, nudging Fletch aside. Izzy kicked, slamming her foot into the bars and exploding the cell door outward. The door swung into the knights, and a dozen tumbled back, collapsing into a bony heap.

But many, many skeletal knights still remained.

"Time to fight!" Izzy said. She dashed out of the cell, raced toward the wall, reached for the mace, gripped it, and—

ZAP!

The mace clanked to the floor, and Izzy was rocketed across the room. Her hair shot up, shocked straight. "Aw, man. Really? Again?" she said in a dazed voice.

From the cell, Fletch shouted, "What happened?"

"The weapons must have become infused with bits of the Forbidden Power," Izzy called. "I can't use them!"

Fletch gulped, then shook his head. "But I can't fight! You know that!"

Dodging a skeletal knight's swinging sword, Izzy said, "You have to!"

Fletch saw four knights charging toward Izzy—and realized he had no choice. "Into the cell!" Fletch said.

"Again?" she cried out.

"Again!"

"Argh. I keep missing out on the action!" Izzy groaned. Fletch sprinted out of the cell while Izzy retreated into it. She slammed the door shut just as four knights crashed into the bars. A blade slashed through. Izzy spun, dodging it, then clanged the lock shut.

Izzy wasn't sure whether she should be relieved or annoyed that she was, for the second time in about two minutes, locked inside a cage.

Fletch sprinted past one knight's outstretched bony hand and leapt for the wall. He grabbed hold of a sword, feeling fantastic, heroic—and then it clonked to the ground, bringing him with it.

"Oof!" Fletch said, groaning. "It's heavy! I think I hurt my back . . ."

"Go for something lighter!" Izzy called.

A lone arrow lay on the floor. *An arrow,* Fletch wondered. *Again?*

With no other choice, he picked it up. The weapon tingled in his hand. He suddenly felt power rushing through him. A playful grin danced across his face, and a sense of calm overcame him. He felt in control as he wielded the energy-infused weapon.

It was different than in the Combatition, with Zilgo. This time he didn't *think* about fighting. He simply did it. He followed his instincts—*the feeling.* With every swing of the arrow, a knight collapsed into a pile of bone.

Izzy watched her fighting friend with astonishment— but only for a moment. She had to do *something.* She scooped a small stone up from the floor and scrambled up the side of the cell. Peering through the barred window, outside, she spotted the Rogul—still waiting behind the tree.

"Come here!" she shouted.

Slowly, the Rogul drifted out from behind the tree.

"Come here!" she shouted again.

The Rogul shook his head.

"Fletch needs you!"

Izzy's eyes suddenly went wide. The Rogul had just crumbled. The entire thing simply fell apart.

Izzy gasped. "What the—"

Across the field, the stones came rolling. The grass swayed as the rocks bowled forward, toward the small barred window.

Izzy suddenly realized what was about to happen. She leapt back—just as the pile of rocks came sifting through the barred window and crashing to the floor.

"Fletch!" Izzy shouted, her voice quivering. "Something *really* weird is happening with the Rogul! It turned into, like, a pile of rocks!"

But Fletch didn't hear his friend. He heard nothing but his own heartbeat, slamming in his eardrums as he battled. He had demolished seven knights.

His body heaved.

He lifted the arrow and jabbed and jabbed, but he had nothing left. His arms felt like spaghetti.

The remaining knights cackled. Their weapons were pointed at him. Fletch gulped, looking from undead face-to-undead-face.

But then Fletch heard the sound of tumbling stone. Glancing down, he saw rocks and pebbles coming through the cell bars. He took two confused steps back, just as the pebbles began to join together, forming the massive Rogul statue—rising to full size. And in only moments—

KRAK!

SLAM!

BASH!

POW!

The Rogul turned the remaining skeletal knights to scattered bone. The knights crumbled and bent and twisted, and armor was strewn across the floor.

"*GRUNT.*"

Fletch grinned. "Right back at ya!"

A moment later, Fletch had unlocked the cell. "Okay, Izzy," he said. "It's time to get that Forbidden Power back!"

CHAPTER ELEVEN

Fletch and Izzy snuck back up the spiral staircase. The Rogul hovered behind them. Fletch peered into the throne room. The bone throne was empty, and the room appeared deserted.

Fletch swallowed: The Forbidden Power was gone.

Suddenly, a flash of movement—candlelight flickered. Fletch and Izzy both looked up just in time to see a skeletal knight leaping from the chandelier. The knight slammed into Izzy.

"Get off me, you undead head!" Izzy shouted as the knight dug his bony hand into her shoulder. They staggered across the room, almost like they were dancing.

"Izzy!" Fletch cried out, and charged after them. But it was too late; he saw it happening. Their struggle had them careening toward the rotten wall and then—

KRUNCH!

The boards splintered as Izzy and the knight slammed into the wall, crashing right *through it*.

Fletch dashed, heart pounding, and peered through the wall. Looking up at him, grinning, was Izzy. Izzy and the knight had landed in the yard—and the skeletal knight had crumbled.

"Bone butt here broke my fall," Izzy called up.

"Get back here!" Fletch shouted.

Izzy knocked a stray bone from her shoulder as she got to her feet. "You keep going!" she called. "There's something I need to do."

Before Fletch had a chance to protest, Izzy was sprinting across the lawn. He watched her go, then glanced around the throne room.

His eyes focused on a hall that appeared to lead to the strange mansion's second wing.

And then he sensed it. Fletch could *feel* the power there, calling to him.

Fletch and the Rogul crept down a long hall, then up a seemingly endless series of steps, finally exiting in the mansion's second wing. It was a maze of halls and rooms. Tapestries were hung along the walls. The floors creaked with every step. Candleholders on the wall cast dancing red-orange light. The light mixed with the blue glow of the Rogul, turning the entire labyrinth a ghostly teal.

Fletch glanced back, hoping to see Izzy come speeding up the stairs. She would crack a joke and put him at ease—maybe even stop his heart from pounding out of his chest. But she didn't come: It was only Fletch, the Rogul, and—*somewhere in this maze*—Baron von Bludgeonous. Fletch gripped the arrow tighter.

Fletch felt the Forbidden Power radiating from somewhere close. He continued through the maze, passing haunting old paintings and bizarre artifacts. *The feeling* grew stronger, and as Fletch slowly turned the next corner, he expected to come up on Baron von Bludgeonous and the Forbidden Power.

But it was a dead end.

Fletch didn't understand.

The feeling hadn't led him astray. Not yet.

Fletch stepped closer to the wall that marked the sudden end of the hall. He saw it had a slight curve to it. The curve made Fletch think of the huge spire they had seen from outside. Fletch had lost his sense of direction inside the maze, but could the spire be here? Beyond this curved wall?

"Well, what do you think?" Fletch asked the Rogul.

"*GRUNT.*"

Peering closer, Fletch saw dull, barely visible light leaking through cracks in the curved wall and from the base, along the floor.

The Forbidden Power.

Fletch took a deep breath, then gently placed a hand on the wall. The instant he did—

WHAM!

As if pulled by some unseen force, the wall crashed open, revealing the spire. Baron von Bludgeonous towered in the center of the large, round room. He had one hand on the Forbidden Power, and he seemed to be drawing the power from it—his body glowed. Baron von Bludgeonous had grown even larger and more terrifying. Power rushed through his bones. Fletch realized the Forbidden Power was making him stronger . . .

Baron von Bludgeonous' eyes burned with electrical purple light—the color of the Forbidden Power. Fletch felt the chilling pierce of Baron von Bludgeonous' stare. The undead knight was the embodiment of fear. In that instant, Fletch felt that Baron von Bludgeonous was *all fear*—every anxious, agitated, apprehensive, and just straight-up *scared* moment of Fletch's life.

"You have interrupted me," Baron von Bludgeonous growled.

Fletch gritted his teeth, choked back the fright, and buried his lifetime of fear. He took a slow but steady stride forward—raising the arrow and pointing it at the foul knight. "I'm taking that power back to the academy," Fletch said, his voice firm.

"You are not."

"It belongs in a museum!" Fletch barked. "Or, I mean, y'know, with Merlok or whatever."

The blue energy in Baron von Bludgeonous' eyes danced, questioning the boy. He gripped the Forbidden Power tighter. "An army of flesh-and-blood knights

couldn't pry this from my cold, undead hands," Baron von Bludgeonous croaked.

"I don't have an army with me, but I do have a giant stone statue dude," Fletch said. He quickly sprang sideways, revealing the Rogul.

The Rogul hovered steadily behind Fletch, but only for a second—then he was roaring forward, slamming into Baron von Bludgeonous. The knight's tight grip on the power was undone, and the shield dropped to the floor.

"You're a monster," Fletch said.

"No," Baron von Bludgeonous said. "I am a knight—a knight who should be a *king*. And I will take that throne."

Bludgeonous rushed forward, swinging a mighty hand. The Rogul swiveled to the side, shielding Fletch—but the undead knight's blow was infused with energy. The punch propelled the Rogul back, sending him spinning through the entranceway. Electricity crackled.

"Looks like your stone guardian is gone," Baron von Bludgeonous said. "And all you have is a single arrow."

Bludgeonous' eyes flashed red, and Fletch was suddenly blasted across the spire! He slammed into the wall. Fletch's arrow—his only weapon—clattered to the floor. Baron von Bludgeonous raised his mighty lance in one hand and lifted the Forbidden Power with the other—

"Hey, ya big crummy knight!"

Fletch whirled to see Izzy, marching down the hall, holding Ned Knightley's Silver Sword of Silverness. "Recognize this?"

Baron von Bludgeonous saw the legendary sword— and it rocked him. His entire body shuddered, bones and armor rattling, and he staggered back. "N-n-no. It can't be. Ned Knightley's—"

"That's right," Izzy said. "The Silver Sword of Silverness! The sword of the most righteous knight of all time. A good knight. The opposite of you!"

The blade shimmered, shining silver. Baron von Bludgeonous cowered, inching back. He dropped his lance and threw a hand up to block the light.

"Fletch, get the power!" Izzy shouted.

Fletch didn't hesitate. He rushed forward, grabbing hold of the Forbidden Power, struggling to yank it free. But Baron von Bludgeonous still had some fight left in him. His bony hands held it tight.

The tablet shook, and Vicious Voltage pulsed. "I have hunted too long for this to let a boy take it from me!" Bludgeonous growled.

Fletch glanced at his arrow, lying on the ground. "Not just a boy," he said, lifting the arrow off the floor. "A knight-in-training!"

The moment Fletch lifted the arrow, a beam of Vicious Voltage leapt from the shield and into the arrow's tip. The arrow sparked and glowed as electrical energy flowed back and forth, and it rushed from Fletch's arrow into the shield, and from the shield into Fletch's arrow.

Baron von Bludgeonous gripped the shield, hugging it tight. "You can't have it!" he howled.

Fletch felt the arrow-wand shaking harder and harder. He threw his second hand over it, trying to control it. But he couldn't . . .

Over the thunderous crackling sound of lightning, Fletch managed to scream, "Izzy! Get down!"

Glancing back, Fletch saw Izzy dive for cover. And just in time . . .

Fletch gripped the pulsing, jumping arrow-wand and stepped closer to the tablet.

The walls clattered, and the floor cracked. Fletch stepped closer still.

The entire world seemed to shake.

Baron von Bludgeonous glared at Fletch. "We'll meet again, boy," he growled. "I promise."

Fletch stepped even closer, finally pressing the arrow against the shield. A blindingly bright light filled the room. The walls splintered, and the ceiling began to crack and crumble. And then—

KRAKA-BOOM!

CHAPTER TWELVE

When the smoke cleared, Fletch saw the walls had been destroyed and the roof of the spire was gone. And Baron von Bludgeonous was gone with it.

Izzy hurried to the smoldering edge and peered down. The Pegasus' stable was empty. "Disappeared," Izzy said. "Both of them."

"Not all that's missing," Fletch said, glancing around. "The Forbidden Power is gone. It just *vanished*."

A sudden, deafening rumble startled Fletch.

"It's only the Fortrex," Izzy said happily.

"The huh?" Fletch asked.

The Fortrex—the NEXO KNIGHTS team's heavily armed, heavily armored rolling castle—came to a loud, shuddering stop in the street. A drawbridge door opened, and Clay Moorington came striding down the ramp. A moment later, Lance Richmond appeared, followed by Aaron Fox, Macy Halbert, and Axl.

Axl sniffed the air. "Mmm. Burning. Smells like barbeque!"

"What happened here?" Macy asked as she eyed the dark mansion.

Up high, in the spire, Fletch beamed at Izzy. "Go ahead . . ."

With a huge smile, Izzy leaned forward, cupped her hands around her mouth, and shouted, "*We* happened!"

The knights all gazed up at the smoldering, decimated spire. Lance squinted. "Um, is that my *sister*?"

"Hey, bro!" Izzy called out. "Yep, it's me. And this here is Fletch. He just saved the kingdom."

"She helped!" Fletch shouted.

"Barely! Mostly him!"

Fletch smiled and shook his head—but he didn't bother to argue . . .

The Fortrex rumbled through the streets, carrying Fletch and Izzy back to the Knights' Academy.

Fletch, Izzy, and the NEXO KNIGHTS heroes all sat in the Fortrex's command center—and everyone but Izzy was speechless. She was just finishing telling them all that happened: the Forbidden Power, the catacombs, the Combatition, the attack on the academy, the race to the manor, the battle in the dungeon, and the villain Baron von Bludgeonous.

Fletch had barely said a word while Izzy told the tale. Instead, he steadily devoured every bite of food that the Squirebot Chef Éclair brought him. He felt like he hadn't eaten in days. The Rogul was behind him, quietly hovering.

However, Izzy *had* left out a few minor—but very important—details in her telling of the adventure. She didn't mention Fletch's *feeling*, or the details of how he had brought the Rogul statue to life. And when she got to the part about Fletch's duel with Baron von Bludgeonous, she glanced eagerly at her friend, raising her eyebrows, hoping to get him to spill the details.

But Fletch only smiled, shrugged, and chomped into a turkey leg.

"Well," Izzy said. "I guess that's it, then. Any questions?"

The knights all stared at Izzy for a moment, then slowly turned and looked at Fletch. They didn't seem to know just what, exactly, to think of the first-year student. Fletch wished someone would say something . . .

Someone did.

Merlok 2.0.

At that very moment, Merlok appeared, his holographic image materializing on the pedestal at the center of the room. "I hope I'm not too late!" he exclaimed. "Did I miss anything?"

"Only the whole story!" Macy said.

"Well, could you please start from—" Merlok began, and then suddenly burst out, "Oh my! A Rogul! In the Fortrex! There is a *Rogul* in the *Fortrex*!"

But before Fletch could explain, Merlok *again* exclaimed. "Oh, but *of course* there is a Rogul here!" he said. "A Forbidden Power was discovered, and a Rogul would have been guarding it . . . I did explain that earlier, didn't I?"

"Yes," Fletch said, biting back a smile.

Merlok continued. "And the Rogul is the loyal protectorate of the one who *releases* the power . . ."

"Wait," Fletch said. "So is this guy just going to follow me around forever? Don't get me wrong—he's great. It just, ah, could get awkward. Sometimes. If you catch my drift?"

Aaron chuckled at that.

"Yes, yes," Merlok said. "Fletch, you and I should speak further. We must discuss the Rogul—and, I believe, a great many other things . . ."

Izzy looked excitedly at Fletch.

"Okay with me," Fletch said with a smile.

"Merlok, I have one question," Clay said, standing up. Fletch saw that the knight was gripping the back of his chair very tightly. "This Forbidden Power. Was it destroyed?"

Merlok glanced from Clay to Fletch. "What happened, at the end?" he asked.

Fletch shrugged. "I—I wish I knew. It was just an explosion of energy . . ."

"And let me say, from the outside—oh man—it looked *awesome*," Izzy said with a wide smile.

After a moment, Merlok said, "Then, yes, I suspect it was destroyed. But I have not considered the Forbidden Powers for a great many years. I must do some thinking. And some parsing of my memories. Fletch, you will come see me, yes?"

"Of course," Fletch replied.

"Good. Very good!" Merlok exclaimed. "And now—I think I shall nap."

With that, Merlok blipped out.

Fletch's heart was racing. He knew Merlok might be

the one person who could tell him just what the deal was with *the feeling*. And maybe, possibly, *hopefully* Merlok could help keep him from turning evil.

Not turning evil *would* be nice, Fletch thought.

It was nearly dawn when the Fortrex rumbled to a stop at the academy gates. Fletch breathed a huge sigh of relief when he saw that the academy was brightly lit up—apparently, Ava had gotten everything working again.

The Fortrex's drawbridge ramp thudded to the ground, and Lance hurried them out. "All right, sis," he said. "Back to school. Don't go getting a big head. There's only room for one superstar in this family."

"Yeah, yeah," Izzy said, flashing her brother a smirk.

Fletch gulped. He saw that Principal Brickland was standing at the academy entrance—and he didn't look pleased.

Fletch felt a hand on his shoulder. It was Clay. Just looking at him, feeling his presence—Fletch immediately understood why he was the leader of the NEXO KNIGHTS team. Clay's face was strong but kind, and Fletch felt proud to know he was following in his footsteps, as a knight. "Izzy never mentioned your last name," Clay said.

"It's Bowman," Fletch said, suddenly feeling very shy. "Fletcher. Fletcher Bowman."

Clay rubbed his thick, square jaw. "Bowman, eh?" he said curiously. "I don't believe I know that name. Where is your family from?"

Fletch swallowed. "Well, I actually—um—I actually don't know. I'm an orphan . . ." Fletch said, and he felt his eyes drop to the ground.

"An orphan?" Clay asked.

Fletch blushed. "Yeah . . ."

Clay gave Fletch a hearty pat on the back. So hearty that Fletch almost coughed up a lung. "I'm an orphan, too," Clay said.

Fletch couldn't hold back the grin. Clay wasn't from some famous family? The greatest, bravest, most knightliest knight in the land was *also* an orphan?

"You two did well. We're all impressed. And Principal Brickland, he'll do his best to hide it—but he'll be impressed also. Trust me, I know," Clay said with a sly grin.

Fletch smiled, and with that, Fletch, Izzy, and—of course!—the Rogul headed back to the academy. They were barely through the gate when Principal Brickland barked, "My office! Now!"

They spent nearly an hour in Brickland's office, listening to him rant and rave and watching him stomp this way and that. He pounded his desk so many times that Fletch was amazed it didn't break in two.

It was just a bluster of words and phrases: "Tremendous danger!" "Unbelievable!" "Outrageous!"

Finally, when his face had turned so red he was practically purple, Principal Brickland collapsed into his chair. "I don't know how you did it . . ."

Brickland shook his head and stared at them—and behind all the frustration and the screaming—Fletch thought he saw just the slightest bit of a smile on Brickland's face. Brickland caught himself, his mouth returning to a hard frown.

"These little adventures?" he barked. "*Don't* make them a habit. You understand?"

"Yes, sir," Fletch said.

"And that *thing*," he said, waving at the Rogul. "I don't want to see it in the classrooms, I don't want to see it in the cafeteria, and I *certainly* don't want to see it out on the training grounds. It's got the smell of magic to it. Foul. *Evil*, if you ask me."

After his whirlwind first few days at Knights' Academy, Fletch was eager to just be a regular, normal student. But that proved hard. The entire academy was abuzz, and the students were still talking about what Fletch did at the Combatition and how it resulted in a full academy power outage (which everyone thought was kind of awesome).

Principal Brickland had been able to keep *most* of the adventure a secret: None of the students knew about Baron von Bludgeonous or the battle at the mansion, and Fletch's Forbidden Power eruption at the Combatition had been blamed on a Novix malfunction.

But one thing could not be kept a secret: the Rogul.

The other students all seemed to think the Rogul was very odd, but happily for Fletch, they thought it was odd in a *good* way. For a full week, Fletch had a steady stream of visitors to his dormitory, eager to get a glimpse of the strange creature. And Fletch, though still quite shy, found that the Rogul was, actually, quite the conversation piece.

The only student who *didn't* think the Rogul was particularly great was Ethan Zilgo. After the confrontation in the Hall of Knights, Zilgo seemed even more determined to prove something odd was up with Fletch.

"Wait, he said what?" Izzy exclaimed.

It was third period, and Fletch and Izzy were walking the Hall of Knights. In Combo Power Class, Professor Ottofae had mistakenly beamed down three dozen wild turkeys, so everyone had been dismissed early. Fletch and Izzy decided to visit the hall. It was their first time back since they plucked Ned Knightley's

Silver Sword of Silverness from the pedestal and entered the catacombs.

"Yeah," Fletch said with a sigh. "Zilgo said he's going to prove I'm a 'fraud.' Whatever that means."

"He's lousy. Beak, too."

Fletch simply shrugged. As they walked, he ran his hand along the sculptures. He was being quieter than usual, and Izzy noticed. "What's on your mind?" she finally asked.

"Magic," Fletch said, softly. "I've heard it twice now: Anyone who has magic abilities turns to evil. I'm worried that, well, you know—*the obvious*."

Izzy shook her head. "You've got a good heart, buddy. Too good to be corrupted."

Fletch shrugged. "Maybe. Hopefully after talking to—"

"Baron von Bludgeonous!" Izzy burst out.

"What? Huh? Why would I talk to *him*?" Fletch asked.

Izzy shook her head. "No, I mean, it's Baron von Bludgeonous—right there!"

"What?" Fletch exclaimed, eyes darting about.

And then he saw that it was true.

Baron von Bludgeonous *was* right there. Well, a sculpture of him at least. It was one of the many sculptures in the great hall. It showed the knight—young,

handsome, *alive*—not just bone. He sat atop a horse and carried a lance.

And there, on the sculpture, in bronze letters: *Baron von Bludgeonous, a Knight to be Admired, a Student to be Remembered.*

"Not only was Baron von Bludgeonous a knight, he was a student here!" Izzy said. "At the academy!"

"It doesn't say anything about him being heir to the throne, though," Fletch said.

Izzy nodded. "And that would be a big thing not to mention."

"Most important," Fletch said, "now that we know he was a student—maybe we can figure out how to defeat him once and for all . . ."

MAX BRALLIER is the author of more than thirty books and games, including the middle-grade series The Last Kids on Earth.

He writes children's books and adult books, including the pick-your-own-path adventure *Can YOU Survive the Zombie Apocalypse?* He is the creator and writer of Galactic Hot Dogs, a sci-fi middle-grade series from Aladdin. He writes for licensed properties including *Adventure Time, Regular Show, Steven Universe,* and *Uncle Grandpa.*

Under the pen name Jack Chabert, he is the creator and author of the Eerie Elementary series for Scholastic and the author of the *New York Times* bestselling *Poptropica: Vol 1: Mystery of the Map.*

In the olden days, he was a game designer for the virtual world Poptropica and worked in the marketing department at St. Martin's Press. Max lives in New York City with his wife, Alyse, who is way too good for him. Follow Max on Twitter @MaxBrallier.